THE VIRGIN'S
SICILIAN
PROTECTOR

THE VIRGIN'S SICILIAN PROTECTOR

CHANTELLE SHAW

MILLS & BOON

First published in Great Britain 2018
by Mills & Boon, an imprint of HarperCollins*Publishers*
1 London Bridge Street, London, SE1 9GF

Large Print edition 2019

© 2018 Chantelle Shaw

ISBN: 978-0-263-08220-3

MIX
Paper from
responsible sources
FSC™ C007454

This book is produced from independently certified FSC™ paper to ensure responsible forest management. For more information visit www.harpercollins.co.uk/green.

Printed and bound in Great Britain
by CPI Group (UK) Ltd, Croydon, CR0 4YY

For Rosie and Rob.
You are both amazing.
Just keep swimming!

CHAPTER ONE

THE PICTURE SPLASHED across the front page of the newspaper was damning. Arianna focused her bleary gaze on the photograph of herself, almost spilling out of a tiny bikini top and swigging champagne from a bottle, and shuddered.

Once she would not have given a damn that she'd made the headlines yet again. But that had been before she'd had an epiphany on her twenty-fourth birthday, just over a year ago, and realised that nothing she did would make her father take any notice of her. The only thing he was interested in, besides making money, was controlling her, as he had controlled her mother.

Arianna regularly spent the summer at the family villa in Positano and, although she'd never bothered to learn the language properly, she'd picked up enough Italian to be able to translate the paragraph beneath the newspaper picture.

The return of the Brat Pack!

Once again the offspring of many of Europe's wealthiest families have flocked to the Amalfi coast to spend the summer partying.

Heiress Arianna Fitzgerald was clearly enjoying herself with close friend, reality television star Jonny Monaghan, aboard his luxury yacht.

Arianna is the daughter of billionaire fashion designer Randolph Fitzgerald and has been famously described in the British press as 'the most privileged and pointless person on the planet'.

That particular comment had been reprinted so often that Arianna was bored of reading it. She dropped the newspaper down on the patio tiles, feeling too disorientated to wonder who had left it where she was bound to see it, and rolled over onto her back, trying to remember why she had spent the night on a sun lounger by the pool. Her head was thumping and her mouth was parched. She had no recollection of how she had come to be on Jonny's boat, or how she had arrived at Villa Cadenza. Nor could she remember tying a sarong around her to cover up the miniscule gold bikini that had been a regrettable impulse buy when she had been in Australia.

God, she felt awful. But it couldn't be a hangover because she'd barely drunk any alcohol. She wondered if someone could have spiked the bottle of champagne she'd taken a sip out of. Jonny and his crowd—who had once been *her* crowd—used cocaine and other so-called recreational substances to alleviate their terminal boredom. But, although Arianna had partied as hard and as frequently as her peers, she'd never taken drugs, because she had seen the devastating effects they'd had on some of her friends.

As she lay there trying to summon the energy to get up off the lounger and go into the house, she heard footsteps on the marble tiles, and the aroma of coffee assailed her senses.

Good old Filippo. The butler had been kind to Arianna when she'd been a child—unlike most of the temporary nannies her father had employed to look after her during the school holidays. She had attended an exclusive English boarding school but her refusal to accept any kind of authority had led to her being expelled when she'd been fifteen.

Filippo was one of the few people who had not seemed to disapprove of her when she'd been a surly pre-teen and then a rebellious young adult. She could also testify that the butler's secret recipe for a hangover cure worked. But what she craved right now was strong black coffee.

The footsteps halted and Arianna frowned. It was true she had never paid any attention to Filippo's footwear before, but she was sure he did not usually wear heavy-duty black leather boots. Or faded denim jeans. She lifted her gaze and discovered that the waistband of the jeans sat low on a pair of lean hips, above which was a black T-shirt stretched tight over a flat stomach and a broad, impressively muscular chest.

The man, who was definitely too tall to be Filippo, was carrying a tray. Had her father employed a new butler? She craned her neck so that her gaze reached the man's face and her heart crashed against her ribs.

'Who are you? And where's Filippo?' Her voice sounded husky because her throat was dry, not because the stranger's stunning good looks had taken her breath away, she assured herself.

'My name is Santino Vasari. I'm your new bodyguard.' The deep rumble of his voice, as sensuous as dark molasses, had a peculiar effect on Arianna's insides. 'Your father said he would let you know that he had hired me.'

'Oh, yes.' The fog around her brain was clearing and she remembered the text she'd received from her father yesterday when she had arrived in London on a long-haul flight from Sydney. Stupidly, her heart had leapt when she'd seen Randolph's name flash up on her phone's screen. She'd wondered if he'd missed her while she had been in Australia for six months. But the message had simply said that a bodyguard would meet her at Villa

Cadenza, and that Santino Vasari was an ex-soldier who had turned to private protection work after he'd left the army.

His incredible physique certainly suggested that he had been in the armed forces. Arianna licked her dry lips with the tip of her tongue and flushed when his gaze focused on her mouth. She felt at a disadvantage sprawled on the sun bed while his eyes roamed over the silk sarong that had become bunched up around her thighs before he continued a leisurely inspection of her bare legs. She was used to attracting attention. Indeed, she had spent much of the past decade seeking notoriety and scandal. But something about Santino Vasari and her unexpected reaction to him made her sit up and swing her legs over the side of the lounger.

She winced as the movement exacerbated her pounding headache and the smirk on Santino's lips sent a sizzle of temper through her.

'I did not ask for a bodyguard. You have had a wasted journey here,' she said abruptly. Her cut-glass English accent was as sharp as a razor. 'I don't want you, Mr Vasari.'

'Is that a fact?' There was disbelief in his

lazy drawl. An arrogant, almost cocky confidence that every woman who laid eyes on him wanted him. His self-assurance was probably not misplaced, Arianna acknowledged. 'Handsome' did not come close to describing the ruggedly masculine beauty of his chiselled features: the slashing lines of his cheekbones that emphasised the harsh angles of his face and the square, worryingly determined jaw, covered with dark stubble the same colour as the almost black hair that curled rebelliously over his collar.

Santino Vasari did not appear to be fazed by her frosty attitude. He strolled towards her, moving with a loose-limbed grace that reminded Arianna of a prowling lion—silent, purposeful and decidedly dangerous. His manner was relaxed but his eyes—startlingly green eyes that gleamed as brightly as peridots—were watchful and unsettlingly perceptive.

Her heart gave another hard kick in her chest when he dropped his gaze to the swell of her breasts. Heat surged through her. She felt her nipples pucker but managed to resist the urge to glance down to see if they were visible through her bikini top. No other man had ever had such a potent effect on her. Not one. She'd come to the conclusion some time ago that she had a low sex drive—or maybe she was frigid, as an ex-boyfriend had told her when she had refused to have sex with him.

Arianna lifted her chin and forced herself to meet Santino's mocking look with cool indifference. But when he placed the tray on a low table, before he pulled a chair up close to her sun bed and sat down, her heartbeat accelerated. Her senses seemed more acute and she breathed in the spicy sandalwood scent of his aftershave carried on the warm, early morning air.

'You see, Arianna…' he murmured, and she quickly tore her gaze from his mouth. 'May I call you Arianna? "Miss Fitzgerald" is frankly a bit of a mouthful when we are going to be spending a lot of time together.'

'The hell we are!'

He ignored her angry outburst. 'Whether you like it or not your father has hired me to be your protection officer, which means that

I will accompany you every time you leave the house.'

She drummed her long, perfectly manicured nails on the arm of the sun lounger. 'Why has Randolph developed a sudden urge to protect me when he has never shown any concern for me before? And why does he think I need protecting while I'm here? Positano has a low crime rate, and I'm well known in the area. I've been coming here every summer since I was a child.'

'You certainly announced your arrival in Amalfi,' Santino said in a dry tone. He picked up the newspaper. 'You were still asleep when I brought you a copy of today's paper. The picture of you fooling around with your sailor boyfriend made the front page of many of the English and European tabloids, as well as the local press here on the Amalfi Coast. Anyone who wants to find you won't have to look very hard.'

Arianna shrugged to hide her discomfiture that she'd been unaware of his presence while she'd slept. It made her feel vulnerable, somehow, knowing that he was the only man who had ever seen her asleep. 'I don't suppose any-one will be looking for me. Most of my friends are aware that I spend the summer in Positano.'

She wondered why Santino had sounded terse, but as she stared at the newspaper she suddenly understood. 'I'm not stupid, Mr Vasari. I am aware of the reason why my father hired you.'

She thought that he tensed, although she couldn't be sure. His eyes narrowed on her face but his tone bordered on uninterested as he murmured, 'And what reason is that?'

'Randolph employed you to make sure that I keep out of trouble and out of the papers, didn't he?'

'You have a well-documented history of getting into trouble.' Santino flicked his gaze back to the newspaper photo, and the look of contempt that crossed his hard features filled Arianna with an emotion that she was startled to realise was shame.

She had never cared what other people thought of her, or at least that was what she had tried to convince herself. The scathing words of the headmistress who had expelled her from her school—that she would amount to nothing in life unless she changed her attitude—still stung ten years later. But, Arianna assured herself, she absolutely did not care what a man who made a living from looking menacing, and who was probably all brawn and no brains, thought of her.

'Drinking yourself to oblivion and flaunting your body like a hooker seems like pretty stupid behaviour in my opinion,' Santino Vasari said, and something in his tone made her feel as small and insignificant as she'd felt all those years ago in the headmistress's office.

Her jaw dropped. No one had ever spoken to her quite so bluntly before, and the thought struck her that if her father *had* criticised her just once it would have been an indication that he cared about her. But Randolph's lack of interest had led to her running wild throughout her teenage years and she'd behaved like the spoilt brat that the tabloids, and the odious man who was sitting too close to her and invading her personal space, believed she was.

'I did not ask for, nor am I the least bit in-

terested in, your opinion,' she informed Santino icily.

The glitter in his green eyes sent a frisson
of excitement through her when she realised
that he was struggling to control his temper.
At least she made him feel *something*—which
she had never achieved with her father.

'I expected you to arrive at Naples airport on
a flight from London yesterday. But, when I
went to meet you, you didn't show up,' he said
curtly. 'How did you get to Positano?'

She shrugged. 'At Heathrow I bumped into a
friend, Davina, who was about to fly to Amalfi
on her father's company jet and she invited me
to go with her.' It was all coming back to Arianna now. The private jet had landed at an air-
field near to the Amalfi coast and Davina had
arranged to join Jonny and a group of friends
on his yacht *Sun Princess*.

By then it had been something like thirty-
nine hours since Arianna had left Sydney and
she had hardly eaten or drunk anything in that
time. She'd been too tired to argue when Jonny
had pulled her onto the yacht, saying that he
would take her along the coast to Positano.

All she had wanted to do was sleep, but with a party in full swing it had been impossible. At least sunbathing on the deck had allowed her to close her eyes, and she had worn the gold bikini for the first time without realising how inadequately the tiny triangles of material covered her breasts.

When someone had passed her a bottle of champagne, she'd taken a sip to quench her thirst. It was bad luck that just then a speedboat had raced alongside the yacht and the paparazzi on board had taken the photograph which had made it onto the front page of the newspapers.

She glanced at Santino's arresting face. He was not handsome in a pretty sense, unlike some of the male models with whom she had worked on fashion shoots. Featuring on the front covers of upmarket glossy magazines was her only claim to a career, she acknowledged ruefully.

Santino's hard-boned features and powerfully muscular physique exuded a raw masculinity and brooding sensuality that evoked a visceral longing deep in Arianna's pelvis. Her reaction shocked her. For all of her adult life she had flirted and acted the role of a siren, tempting men with her beauty. But she'd never felt desire or chemistry, or whatever this wild heat in her blood was called.

Inexplicably she found herself tempted to explain the true version of what had happened on the yacht. Even more oddly, she considered telling him the truth about herself: that she had finally grown up and wanted to make something good out of her life. But he probably wouldn't believe her, and he would not care anyway. No one ever had. Not her business-obsessed father or her mother who, when Arianna had been a child, had abandoned her for a lover and a new life on the other side of the world.

She watched Santino press the plunger down on the cafetière and pour coffee into the single cup on the tray. Eagerly she reached out her hand to take the cup but he lifted it to his lips and took a long sip.

'It's good coffee,' he murmured appreciatively. 'I suggest you go and get yourself some.

You look as though you could do with a dose of caffeine.'

She flushed, wondering if she looked as bad as he had implied. She ran her fingers through her tangled hair and guessed she looked a wreck after she'd travelled from one time zone to another. Her body clock had gone haywire and she wasn't suffering from a hangover but severe dehydration. 'I assumed that Filippo had asked you to deliver the coffee to me,' she said sharply.

'The butler was whizzing up a concoction of what looked like raw eggs and spinach in a blender.' Santino gave a shrug. 'Filippo told me he usually makes the smoothie to cure your hangover after you've had a heavy night of partying.'

He removed the cover from a plate to reveal Arianna's favourite breakfast that the cook, Ida, always prepared for her of freshly baked rolls and thin slices of ham. Her stomach growled with hunger as she watched him pick up a roll and bite into it. With any luck he would choke, she thought sourly.

'The cook told me she is preparing *agnello*

arrosto con fagioli bianco for dinner—roast lamb with white beans,' he said after he had polished off a second roll. He leaned back in his chair and stretched his arms above his head, causing the hem of his T-shirt to ride up, revealing a strip of his bronzed torso and a sprinkling of black hairs that disappeared beneath the waistband of his jeans. 'I can see I'm going to enjoy staying at Villa Cadenza.'

The glimpse of his taut, tanned abdomen had a strange effect on Arianna's insides and she felt hot all over imagining where his body hair grew more thickly beneath the zip of his jeans. She knew she was blushing, and when she dragged her gaze away from Santino's crotch up to his face the gleam of amusement in his eyes added fuel to her simmering temper.

'You won't be staying here,' she told him furiously. 'I'm going to call my father and put an end to this ridiculous situation.'

Arianna spied her handbag and suitcase on the floor close to the sun bed. Vaguely she remembered that one of the crew on Jonny's yacht had brought her and her luggage to the villa in the early hours of the morning. The front door had been locked and she hadn't wanted to wake the butler so she had slept on a sun bed for the rest of the night.

She dug out her phone and called her father's private number. But inevitably it was his personal assistant, Monica, who answered and gave the usual excuse that Randolph was busy and did not want to be disturbed. 'I'll tell him you phoned and I'm sure he'll be in touch when he has time,' the PA said smoothly, although she must know that Randolph had never in living memory returned one of his daughter's calls.

'I'd like to leave a message for him.' Arianna watched Santino pour out the last of the coffee from the cafetière and gulp it down, and her blood boiled. 'Will you tell my father that I have no need of a bodyguard and I have fired Mr Vasari?' She gave Santino a haughty look. 'He will be leaving Villa Cadenza immediately.'

Santino let his eyes roam over Arianna as she leaned back on the sun bed while she talked on her phone. Her long, tanned legs went on for ever and the silk sarong tied around her body did not hide the fullness of her breasts. Desire spiked sharp and urgent in his groin and he was thankful that the newspaper on his lap hid the betraying bulge beneath his jeans. He had known before he'd agreed to be her bodyguard that she was beautiful, but he had been unprepared for the hunger she aroused in him, the white-hot lust that surged through his veins.

She had recently starred in an advertising campaign for a famous perfume brand and pictures of her on billboards wearing sexy, black lace underwear had ignited a fire inside him. Sex was used indiscriminately by advertisers to sell products, and no doubt every red-blooded male who looked at the photos of Arianna wanted to run their hands over her lush curves and kiss her sensual mouth that was both an invitation and a challenge. But it was a challenge he must ignore, Santino reminded himself.

When he had found her asleep on the sun lounger earlier he'd realised that a camera could not capture the true essence of her beauty. Fine-boned and slender, she'd looked as fragile as a porcelain figurine, and she was quite the loveliest thing he had ever seen. It was those exquisite cheekbones and the delicate perfection of her elfin features, he thought broodily. Photographs did not do justice to the luminosity of her English rose complexion.

She had woken a few minutes ago and her long, curling lashes had swept upwards as she'd surveyed him with her big brown eyes flecked with gold. He told himself he must have imagined he had glimpsed a haunting vulnerability in her gaze. The sulky pout of her mouth was too sensual, too provocative, for her to be anything other than the brazen temptress beloved by the tabloids and gossip columns.

Santino rubbed his hand around the back of his neck to ease a knot of tension in his muscles. His fingers automatically slipped beneath his shirt collar and traced the ten-inch scar from a bullet wound he'd received while he'd been serving in Afghanistan. The bullet had entered just below his shoulder blade and ripped open his body before exiting his neck at the base of his skull. It was incredible that he had survived, and, like the images in his mind of war, the scar would never completely fade. Nor would his guilt.

Eight years ago he had come close to death on a dusty, blood-spattered desert road. His life had been saved by his best friend and fellow SAS member, Mac Wilson, who had dragged him out of the line of fire. But that act of immense bravery had cost Mac his legs when an IED had exploded beneath him.

Restlessly, Santino stood up and walked across the terrace, aware that Arianna's gaze followed him. His thoughts flew back to six months ago when Mac had requested his help to bring down a gang of drug smugglers believed to be responsible for his sister's death. Mac was determined to bring Laura's Italian boyfriend to justice but he had no proof that the man, Enzo, had supplied her with the cocaine which had killed her. Mac had asked Santino to infiltrate the gang who had links to the Calabrian mafia, known as the 'Ndrangheta. He had not needed to remind Santino that he was unable to do so himself because he was confined to a wheelchair.

Working undercover, Santino had discovered that, as well as drug smuggling, the gang had carried out several high-profile kidnappings and been paid millions of pounds of ransom money. Their next target was the English heiress Arianna Fitzgerald. The kidnappers had kept her under surveillance for some time and knew that she spent the summer at her father's villa on the Amalfi coast. Santino had alerted the Italian police, but they had been unable to contact Arianna, so had warned her father of the threat to his daughter.

Santino recalled his meeting with Randolph Fitzgerald a week ago at the billionaire's Kensington home Lyle House.

'You are the best person to protect my daughter when she returns from Australia, Mr Vasari. Name your price. What will it take to persuade you to accept the job of Arianna's bodyguard?'

Santino had been irritated by the other man's arrogant assumption that everything could be bought and everyone had a price, but he guessed that those things were probably true for one of the richest men in England. 'I am not a CPO,' Santino had reminded Randolph. 'I have given you the names of several security agencies who can provide close protection officers and will arrange for your daughter to receive round-the-clock protection.'

'Your training and experience with the SAS gives me confidence that you will be able to keep Arianna safe. After all, it was you who found out that a mafia gang are planning to snatch her from my villa in Positano and demand a multi-million-pound ransom for her release. The Italian police are hunting for the gang but, until they are arrested, the threat to Arianna remains.'

It was true that the in-depth knowledge Santino had amassed about the gang members while he had pretended to be one of them meant he knew how they operated and could be one step ahead of them. But it was also true that he had no desire to babysit a spoilt socialite who, by her own father's admission, was headstrong and difficult.

Even if only a fraction of the reports about Arianna Fitzgerald's party lifestyle were true, she had earned her reputation as a good-time girl. For years her face and her stunning body—invariably poured into figure-hugging dresses—had regularly appeared on the front pages of the tabloids. One social commentator had sarcastically observed that Arianna would turn up to the opening of an envelope if it gave her an opportunity to pose for the cameras.

'I left the army a long time ago and since then I have established a successful career. I don't need a job,' Santino had told her father bluntly. 'It could be months before all the gang members involved in the kidnap plot are apprehended. I can't take that amount of time away from my business interests.'

Randolph nodded. 'I believe your chain of delicatessens under the brand name of Toni's Deli has outlets across the UK and in many European cities. You sold the business eighteen months ago and since then you have concentrated on growing your investment portfolio.'

Noticing Santino's surprise, Randolph had added drily, 'I did my homework about you, Mr Vasari, and I have a proposition that might interest you.'

Despite himself, Santino had been curious.

'I'm guessing that your proposition is dependent on my agreement to protect Arianna?'

'Preparations are underway to float Fitzgerald Design on the stock market and a price has been set at thirty-five pounds per share.' The fashion designer handed Santino a piece of paper. 'The top figure is the valuation of the company, and the figure beneath it is the number of shares I am prepared to give you in return for you taking on the role of my daughter's bodyguard until the kidnap threat is over.'

Santino lifted his brows when he looked at the figures. 'It would cost you a lot less to employ a CPO through a security agency.'

'As I have already stated, I believe you are the best man for the job.' Randolph leaned back in his chair. 'You are no doubt aware that my daughter frequently appears on the front pages of a certain type of newspaper. For some reason Arianna seems to enjoy courting notoriety, but the publicity surrounding her is likely to have brought her to the attention of the gang who intend to kidnap her. An important element of your job will be to shield her from the paparazzi and keep her out of the headlines.'

Randolph was clearly confident that the offer of a significant number of shares in Fitzgerald Design would persuade him to agree to be Arianna's bodyguard, Santino had mused. Why shouldn't he accept the shares as payment for protecting a pampered young woman who, quite frankly, sounded as if she was a pain in the backside?

Originally, he had set aside some time to try and help Mac gain justice—in some form or another—for his sister's death. But Arianna Fitzgerald was being threatened by people who had no respect for life. The 'Ndrangheta were ruthless and Santino did not like to think what they might do to her if they seized her.

Randolph leaned across the desk and, as if he'd read Santino's mind, said, 'I have faith that your SAS training makes you the ideal person to protect my daughter. What do you say?'

There was only one thing that Santino could say. 'All right, I will be Arianna's bodyguard until the gang members have been caught.'

'There is one problem.' Randolph hesitated.

'Arianna must not be told the real reason why I have hired you to be her protection officer.'

When Santino frowned the billionaire quickly continued, 'My daughter is prone to volatile emotions. She has seen various experts—psychologists and so forth.' He gave a dismissive shrug. 'I don't pretend to understand the reason for Arianna's histrionics but a year ago she overdosed and spent several weeks in hospital. I am concerned about how she might react to the news that a mafia gang are planning to kidnap her. For the sake of her emotional stability it will be better if the gravity of the situation is kept from her.'

'I will find it a lot harder to protect Arianna if she is unaware of the danger she is in,' Santino had argued.

'That is why I chose you for the job,' Randolph replied slickly. 'I suggest you allow her to think that the reason I hired you is because the launch of Fitzgerald Design as a public company will attract a huge amount of publicity. I trust that you will keep my daughter safe, Mr Vasari.'

Santino pulled his thoughts back to the present and cursed beneath his breath as he stared at Arianna's scantily clad figure sprawled on the sun bed. His fantasy of undressing her and cradling her pert breasts in his hands would have to remain in his imagination. When he had been in the army a sense of duty and honour had been ingrained in him. Arianna's father had put his faith in him, which meant that the delectable Miss Fitzgerald was definitely off-limits.

CHAPTER TWO

'I'M AFRAID YOU can't dismiss Mr Vasari,' Randolph's PA said in her calm, slightly patronising manner which Arianna found intensely irritating. 'I have his employment contract which both he and your father signed here on my desk.'

'I don't care about any wretched contract.' Too agitated to sit still, Arianna jumped up from the lounger. 'This is intolerable. I don't *want* a bodyguard. Randolph can't force me to have one.'

'Your father told me to inform you that if you do not accept Mr Vasari's protection services then your monthly allowance will be stopped,' the PA said crisply. 'While you are in Positano, Mr Vasari will stay at Villa Cadenza and he will accompany you at all times when you go out.'

For a few moments shock rendered Arianna speechless. It was not the first time her father had used money to try to control her and anger surged like boiling lava through her veins. A year ago she had resolved to start her own fashion-design business so that she could earn her own money and not be reliant on the— admittedly generous—allowance that arrived in her bank account every month. However, her dream of being independent was as yet unfulfilled. Her lack of business skills and serious doubts that her designs were any good had prevented her from turning her dream into reality. Recently she had taken another step towards her goal, but she would need every penny of the money she had inherited from her grandmother to cover the start-up costs of establishing her business. It meant that she would have to rely on the allowance from her father for a little while longer.

But she would not tolerate having her privacy infringed by the constant presence of a bodyguard. Especially not the arrogantly self-assured man who had resumed his seat close to her sun bed. Santino leaned back in the chair and folded his arms behind his head while he trailed his eyes over her and looked unimpressed.

'Unimpressed' was not a reaction Arianna was used to receiving from men. She had attracted male attention since she'd been thirteen, when her body had started to develop from that of a skinny, coltish girl into a curvy young woman with a face and body that men lusted after. At first she had been scared by her power, but as she'd grown older she had learned that she could use feminine wiles to her advantage.

Against her will, her eyes were drawn to Santino's and she glimpsed a fire in his brilliant green gaze that caused heat to unfurl in the pit of her stomach. But she told herself she must have imagined his predatory look when his eyes narrowed and his expression became unfathomable.

She turned away and spoke into her phone in a low tone, conscious that he was within earshot of her conversation. Monica had worked as her father's assistant for years and guarded him fiercely. In truth, Arianna had often felt jealous of the close relationship the other woman had with him. 'Please let me speak to Randolph,' she muttered, feeling a familiar sense of betrayal at her father's indifference.

'I'm sorry. He has meetings for the rest of the day, but I'll let him know that you want to talk to him,' Monica said and ended the call before Arianna could respond.

Angrily she chucked her phone down on the sun bed but it bounced off the cushions and landed on the tiles with an ominous clatter. She picked it up and cursed when she saw a crack across the screen.

'You want to be more careful.' Santino's mocking voice was the last straw and Arianna spun round and glared at him.

'What I *want* is for you to get out of my house!' she snapped, aware that she sounded petulant, but her anger was mixed with a growing sense of panic at the realisation that her father was once again trying to exert his influence over her life.

Santino strolled towards her. His steps were unhurried, yet Arianna sensed that if she bolted towards the house he would move with the deadly speed of a big cat pursuing its prey and catch up with her before she'd gone any distance.

'This isn't your house. Your father owns the villa, and more to the point he pays my wages,' he drawled. 'I have been given instructions from Randolph to stay close to you when you go out shopping or meet your friends in bars or at the beach.'

Santino had not specified that his orders were to monitor her behaviour and prevent her from attracting the paparazzi's attention, but Arianna was certain that was the reason her father had insisted on her having a bodyguard. She knew that Fitzgerald Design was about to be floated on the stock market, and no doubt Randolph was anxious that she did not create any bad publicity before the launch that might affect the share price.

'You're loving this, aren't you?' she accused Santino angrily. Her fingers itched to slap the mocking smile off his handsome face.

He gave her an impatient look. 'I can't say that I relish the prospect of babysitting a spoilt socialite who has no idea how privileged she is.

Your father believes that some of your friends are seriously into the drugs scene and he is concerned about you—'

'My father,' she interrupted him, 'doesn't give a damn about me and he is only concerned with protecting the Fitzgerald Design brand name. It's true that I can't force you to leave, but you will be housed in the staff quarters, and there is no reason for me to have to see you around the villa.'

'Randolph invited me to enjoy the facilities at Villa Cadenza and make myself comfortable. I'll be sleeping in the guest suite next door to your room.' Santino grinned when she glared at him. 'You'll soon get used to me being around and who knows? You might even enjoy my company. I was thinking of having a swim in that amazing infinity pool. Do you want to join me?'

'No,' she said through gritted teeth. She wanted to scream and shout as she'd done as a teenager—when her temper tantrums had been worse than those of a three-year-old, the governess her father had hired after Arianna had been expelled from school had told her.

'The truth, my dear,' Miss Melton had said crisply, 'is that the more you behave like a spoilt brat the less your father will want to have anything to do with you. Mr Fitzgerald is a very busy man and his time is precious.'

The implication had been that Randolph had more important things to do than pay attention to his difficult daughter. Nothing had changed, Arianna thought angrily. Santino Vasari's job was not to protect her but to control her.

He had walked over to the pool and was standing with his back to her, perhaps admiring the clever illusion that the water was pouring over the edge of the terrace. Or maybe he was enjoying the view of the azure sea through the huge glass window in the wall, beyond which was the villa's private beach. There was something so arrogant about his relaxed stance—as if he owned the place—that infuriated her.

Without pausing to think—a trait that had got Arianna into trouble on numerous occasions—she ran up to him and stretched out her hands to shove him into the pool. Her bare feet made no sound on the tiles, yet Santino must have sensed she was behind him, as he leapt out of her path with startling agility for such a big man. With nothing to slow her momentum she teetered on the edge of the pool and let out a yelp as she fell in and the water closed over her head.

She came up coughing and spluttering. The water wasn't cold, but it jolted her to her senses, and for a moment she felt a familiar sense of panic before she realised that she could feel the bottom of the pool beneath her feet. She felt like an idiot for her childish behaviour, and Santino's laughter told her that he shared her opinion. She waded over to the edge of the pool and clambered up the steps, ignoring the hand he held out to assist her.

'I see you changed your mind about having a swim,' he taunted.

Arianna stepped onto the poolside…and discovered that she was no longer wearing the sarong. It must have come loose in the pool and she saw the length of cerise silk floating in the water. 'Go to hell,' she snapped.

'I've already been there.' The amusement had disappeared from his voice. 'Helmand province was a hell on earth that few people, especially someone as privileged as you, could begin to imagine. When I was in Afghanistan I saw good men, some of them my close friends, die in the line of duty.'

'I don't know much about the war in Afghanistan,' she admitted.

'No, I don't suppose you do. Battle reports and casualty figures are not the sort of thing to feature in gossip columns, which I imagine is the only kind of news you read. But I assure you that hell would be a picnic in the park compared to desert warfare.'

Of course he had to be a war hero, Arianna thought, feeling another stab of shame that she had done nothing in her life to be proud of. Being chosen as the face of a perfume advertising campaign was utterly irrelevant compared to Santino risking his life on the battlefield.

She gathered up her long, wet hair in her hands and wrung out some of the water before she flicked it behind her shoulders. Santino made a rough sound, as if he had released his breath slowly, and when Arianna looked at him her gaze was trapped by the hard gleam in his eyes. He was staring at her as if he wanted to devour her and the stark hunger etched on his face evoked something fierce, bright and *electrifying* inside her.

She was supremely conscious that her body was no longer hidden beneath a sarong and her tiny gold bikini was not much more than three triangles of material held together with narrow ties. The action of pushing her hair back had lifted her breasts and, glancing down, she saw the hard points of her nipples jutting provocatively through the clingy, damp bra top.

There was a pile of freshly laundered towels by the side of the pool. Santino strode over, picked up a towel and returned to offer it to Arianna. 'Here, you had better cover yourself up. I can see that you're cold,' he said, resting his gaze deliberately on the betraying hard points of her nipples. The mockery in his voice was mixed with something darker that prickled across her skin and made her breasts feel heavy.

She felt scorched by his glittering gaze, by the heated desire she saw in those green depths. Triumph swept through her with the realisation that he wanted her but she sensed that he resented the attraction he felt for her.

'I'm not cold,' she murmured, ignoring the towel he held out to her. Tipping her head to one side, she regarded him through half-closed lashes, enjoying a sense of feminine power as she gave him a teasing smile, and his jaw hardened. 'I may as well go in the pool with you now that I'm wet.'

She saw his gaze drift over her body, following the droplets of water that she could feel trickling down her stomach to her thong-style bikini pants.

'Are you wearing swim-shorts under your clothes? It doesn't matter if you're not,' she said archly. 'I often sunbathe naked out here on the terrace. I hope that won't make you feel uncomfortable.'

Santino's eyes narrowed. 'I know you like to play games, Arianna, but don't think you can play them with me.' His lips curled sardonically when she opened her eyes wide and gave him a look of pure innocence. 'I've read the tabloid stories about your countless affairs with celebrities, and seen the pictures of you falling out of nightclubs and flaunting that incredible body of yours in revealing clothes that would make a whore blush. You can try all the tricks you like but you won't distract me from doing the job your father hired me to do.'

'And of course the tabloids always tell the truth,' she said abruptly. Her voice was sharper than she'd intended. Santino's scathing tone made her feel grubby and *cheap*. She had spent the best part of ten years trying to punish her father for his lack of interest in her, and she'd actively encouraged the paparazzi's attention with the wild behaviour that had earned her the label of 'spoilt little rich girl'. But the truth was that the only person she had hurt was herself.

There was no reason why the contempt in Santino's eyes should make her feel as if he had peeled away a layer of her skin, leaving her exposed and raw. What right did he have to judge her? He acted like Mr High and Mighty but she had discovered his weakness. How amusing that she was Santino Vasari's Achilles' heel, she thought, hiding her hurt feelings behind a wall of bravado the way she had learned to do since she'd been eleven years old.

She took the towel out of his hand and dropped it onto the floor before she stepped closer to him. A smile played on her lips when he folded his arms across his chest in what could only be described as a defensive gesture, which intrigued her.

'You sound worried, Santino. How do you think I might distract you?' she murmured, running her fingers lightly along his forearm. His skin was like warm silk and beneath it she felt the tensile strength of hard sinews and muscles.

His face hardened, the skin drawn taut over the slashing lines of his cheekbones. 'I'm warning you, Arianna,' he said harshly. 'I'm not one of the pretty boys who flock around you. Don't test my patience too far.'

'How could I do that, I wonder?' she purred. Common sense told her that she should walk into the house right now, taking what was left of her pride with her. But the dismissive tone in Santino's voice clawed at her lifelong sense of insignificance.

Her father had never paid her any attention, but at eighteen she had discovered that the paparazzi swarmed to take pictures of her when she stumbled out of nightclubs looking wild-eyed and the worse for drink. She had been dubbed 'the party princess' by the tabloids and, as her notoriety grew, she was invited to all the best parties. Restaurant openings, theatre first nights, art gallery exhibitions: anyone with a new business to promote included Arianna Fitzgerald on the guest list, knowing that her presence would ensure the event received maximum publicity.

She would show Santino that he could not dismiss her as if she was an irrelevance. He *would* take notice of her. 'Am I testing your patience now?' she asked softly as she trailed her fingers up his arm to his shoulder, feeling his bunched muscles beneath his T-shirt.

His breathing slowed and her heart raced as she continued her exploration, running her fingertips over the rough stubble on his jaw before she traced the sensual shape of his mouth. She pressed her body closer to his and tilted her head up to meet his gaze.

The feral gleam in his eyes caused her heart to lurch. But she could not back down now without making even more of a fool of herself. Cupping his cheek in her palm, she stretched up on her toes and covered his mouth with hers. He made no response. Not a flicker. His arms were still folded across his chest and he was as solid and unmoving as granite. His lips were unyielding, and it occurred to Arianna that in a lifetime of embarrassing herself Santino's rejection was her crowning humiliation.

Desperate to elicit some sort of reaction from him, she nipped his lower lip with her teeth. He made no sound but his chest rose and fell swiftly. 'Don't say I didn't warn you,' he said then, his voice a low growl that resonated through her.

Abruptly he unfolded his arms and clamped his hands on her shoulders. While Arianna was wondering if he intended to push her away from him he jerked her forward so that her soft breasts were pressed up against the hard wall of his chest. His gaze narrowed and she saw fire and fury glinting in his green eyes beneath his thick black lashes. But then his head swooped and he captured her mouth with his in a searing kiss that felt as if he had branded her with his unique potency.

Nothing had prepared her for the devastation he wrought on her mouth or on her soul as he forced her lips apart with the bold flick of his tongue. The heat of his body was dangerously addictive and, when his arms closed around her like bands of steel, trapping her against him, she melted in the inferno.

His kiss was all her fantasies rolled into one. Masterful and merciless, he demanded a response that she was powerless to deny him. She closed her eyes and her senses sang to the slide of his lips over hers and the taste of him on the tip of her tongue. He made her ache *everywhere*.

Needing to be even closer to him, she pressed her pelvis against his. They fitted together like two pieces of a jigsaw. But, before she had time properly to register the shockingly hard bulge of his arousal beneath his jeans, he lifted his mouth from hers at the same time as he withdrew his arms from around her waist and returned his hands to her shoulders.

This time he did push her away from him,

so forcefully that she would have stumbled if he had not tightened his grip on her shoulders, and she feared her bones might snap.

'So, what is your plan, Arianna?' he drawled, no sign in his voice or his sardonic smile of the tumultuous passion that had exploded between them seconds earlier. 'I suppose you think you can accuse me of sexual harassment to give you a legitimate reason to fire me? But it won't wash, princess. It will be your word against mine.'

She sensed the suggestion in his scathing tone that his testimony would hold more credence than hers. After all, she was the darling of the tabloids, renowned for her outrageous behaviour with a string of celebrity lovers. It took every ounce of her willpower not to let him see how much his jibe had hurt, or how vulnerable she felt, still reeling from the kiss that patently had not affected him.

'Of course I wouldn't make a false allegation,' she said stiffly. 'It would be a terrible thing to do when too many women genuinely suffer sexual harassment.'

He looked at her curiously, as if she had surprised him, but then he shrugged. 'So why did you come on to me? I am under no illusions about you, Arianna. I warned you not to play games and I meant it. Your father hired me to be your bodyguard and I will not allow you to distract me. Nor, I should make it clear, do my duties include keeping you entertained with sex. So, if that is what you were hoping for when you kissed me, you're out of luck.'

Arianna wished that the ground would open up and swallow her, but pride came to her rescue and she gave a tinkling laugh as brittle as thin ice on a frozen pond. 'I can hardly bear the disappointment,' she said with a theatrical pout. 'At least you don't need to worry about drowning in the pool, Mr Vasari. That over-inflated ego of yours should help to keep you afloat.'

Santino dropped his hands down to his sides and clenched them into fists as Arianna spun away from him and marched across the terrace. *Well done*, he congratulated himself sarcastically. It was crucial that he gained her trust but all he had succeeded in doing was alienating her.

If he had any sense he would tear his gaze away from the perfect, peachy roundness of her bottom cheeks sassily displayed by her daring choice of swimwear. But his common sense, like his self-control, had gone up in flames when she had put her mouth on his. It occurred to him as he stared at her delectable derriere that it was unlikely she would actually swim in that miniscule bikini and that its purpose instead was to allow her to flaunt her incredible body.

She stepped through the open glass doors into the house and only when she had disappeared from view did he realise that he had been holding his breath. His nostrils flared as he inhaled deeply, but even though she was no longer standing in front of him the lingering scent of her perfume—an intriguing blend of exotic floral notes and something spicier and boldly sensual—inflamed his senses.

Why the hell had he kissed her? Telling himself that technically she had kissed him first did nothing to appease his conscience. He should have pulled his mouth away from hers, but there had been something curiously innocent about the tentative brush of her lips over his that had surprised him. Because he knew all about Arianna Fitzgerald—and 'innocent' was not a word ever associated with her.

The truth, Santino acknowledged grimly, was that his usual, logical thought process had deserted him the instant he'd set eyes on her and he'd felt a jolt of lust in his groin so intense that it had *hurt*. It had felt like a punch, as though he'd been winded and he couldn't catch his breath.

His reaction puzzled him. He was no stranger to beautiful women and he enjoyed an active sex life uncomplicated by emotional entanglements. The women he dated were intelligent professionals—elegant, discreet and unlikely to be plastered over the gutter press half-undressed, he thought, glancing with distaste at the picture of Arianna on the front of the newspaper.

Everything he had heard about her reinforced his belief that she had been over-indulged by her long-suffering father. Every picture of her when she was actually dressed showed that she had expensive tastes in designer clothes, shoes, handbags and fabulous jewellery—presumably all paid for by her doting daddy. In short, Arianna was the kind of woman he despised, but frustratingly his libido did not care that she was a spoilt socialite and his erection was uncomfortably hard pressing against the zip of his jeans.

The turquoise pool looked inviting with sun glinting on the surface. Earlier he'd pulled on a pair of swim-shorts beneath his clothes, thinking there would be time for him to swim while he waited for Arianna to wake up. His jaw clenched as he remembered her remark that she liked to sunbathe naked. Knowing that Arianna was a flirtatious tease did nothing to ease the throb of his arousal. Cursing himself for his weakness, he stripped off his clothes and dived into the pool. He swam as if his life depended on it—thirty lengths, fifty—until his shoulders ached and his chest burned and his rampant libido was subdued.

Later he made a detailed check of the villa's grounds and was concerned by the lack of security. The butler had explained that he locked the front door at night but that Arianna liked to leave her bedroom window open while she slept. The easy access to Villa Cadenza from the private beach was another problem. It would be feasible for kidnappers to climb over the wall and jump down onto the terrace. They could take Arianna at gunpoint through a door in the wall that led to the beach and force her onto a waiting boat without any of the villa's staff noticing or raising the alarm.

As Santino walked into the house he heard the sound of a car's engine. Hurrying back outside, he glimpsed the tail lights of the sports car that he'd seen parked in the garage disappear out of the courtyard. He knew the car belonged to Arianna. Damn her! Her insubordination was infuriating, but he was more furious with himself for not keeping a closer eye on her.

'Did Arianna say where she was going?' he asked Filippo.

The butler shook his head. 'No, but she often visits the beauty salon in the town, and Giovanni's Bar next to the beach is a popular venue where she meets her friends.'

There was also a four-by-four parked in the garage and fortunately the keys were in the ignition. Santino jumped in and fired the engine. The road outside the villa was not overlooked by any other houses for part of the way down the mountain and he was worried that the kidnappers could be waiting to ambush Arianna as she drove away from Villa Cadenza. Moments later he drove out of the gates and was soon hurtling around the hairpin bends, speeding along the road that wound down to the coast.

Despite his simmering temper he could not fail to appreciate the spectacular scenery. The towering grey cliffs were covered with lemon groves that sloped down to the coast. Dominating the skyline was the azure Tyrrhenian Sea sparkling in the bright summer sunshine. The coastline here was similar to his birthplace and the place he thought of as home, Sicily. The difference was that Positano, the same as most of the other towns on the Amalfi coast, had become a chic and expensive tourist destination favoured by the glitterati.

Rounding another bend, the town was revealed in all its picturesque beauty. Pink, peach and terracotta-coloured houses clung perilously to the cliffs and looked as though they were in danger of tumbling into the sea. At the heart of the town stood the Church of Santa Maria Assunta, with its eye-catching dome made of blue, green and yellow tiles. But Santino's eyes were fixed firmly on the silver sports car ahead of him on the road. He saw the car's brake lights flash on as Arianna's progress was impeded by a bus trundling along in front of her.

There was no possibility of overtaking on the narrow road and it was another five minutes before the bus pulled into a bus stop. After another mile or so Arianna turned up a narrow road and Santino followed her. Most of Positano was a pedestrian zone and tourists had to park in one of the garages on the edge of the town. But she drove down a back street where there was parking for local residents and swung her car into a vacant space.

Santino parked behind the open-top sports car and jumped out of the four-by-four. He strode up to the car, leaned over and snatched the key out of the ignition before Arianna had a chance to stop him.

'You really are the most tedious man,' she said languidly, although he sensed the effort it took her to control her temper.

'That's not the impression you gave when you kissed me earlier.' He felt a spurt of satisfaction when she bit her lip, and dismissed the odd idea that her air of vulnerability was not an act.

Her eyes were hidden behind oversized designer sunglasses and he was frustrated that he had no idea what she was thinking. She looked expensively chic in tight white jeans and a blue-and-white-striped Breton top. A red silk scarf kept her long chestnut hair back from her face. Her lips were coated in scarlet gloss and he felt a crazy urge to kiss her until he had removed all traces of lipstick from her mouth.

'Why didn't you tell me you were coming into town?'

'Because I'm going to the beauty salon,' she told him in a bored tone, nodding towards a shop with the name Lucia's Salon over the door. 'I don't need a bodyguard while I'm having my nails done.' She threw her hands up in the air. 'Look around you. There are no paparazzi here to report on my wild behaviour that might embarrass my dear daddy.'

She started to walk towards the salon and glared at him when he fell into step beside her. 'You can't come in. If you insist on staying, you can wait outside, but don't blame me if you get bored, Mr Vasari.'

'I doubt I could ever get bored around you,' he said drily. 'And I thought we had agreed to drop the formality, Arianna.'

She spun round to face him and jabbed her finger into his chest. 'I didn't agree to anything, certainly not to my every move being watched by one of my father's sycophants. I demand that you give me some space.'

Despite his intention to try and win her trust, Santino felt riled by her withering tone. He was tempted to tell her that, far from being her father's sycophant, Randolph had begged him to be her bodyguard.

'You're not really in a position to make demands, are you, Arianna? If I were you I would remember that your father promised to stop your allowance if you refuse my protection. How would you survive?' he taunted. 'It's not as if you have a successful career to fund your extravagant lifestyle. You simply leech off your father.'

'If I want your advice, I'll ask for it,' she snapped, jabbing her finger into his chest a second time.

'Do that again and I guarantee you won't like the consequences.'

'What will you do?' Her husky voice was laced with amusement. 'Will you put me across your knee and spank me?'

Desire kicked hard in his groin at the erotic images her words evoked. His nostrils flared as he inhaled deeply. 'Would you like me to? Are those the kinds of games you like to play?' he drawled, fighting an unbearable temptation to pull her into his arms and cover her sulky mouth with his. She was the most infuriating woman he had ever met, and he could not comprehend why she made him feel more alive than he had felt in years.

He stretched out his hand and removed her

sunglasses. She blinked in the bright sun-shine and the flecks of gold in her brown eyes gleamed with temper.

'Give those back immediately.'

He made a tutting sound. 'Try saying "please". Didn't your parents teach you better manners when you were a child?'

Something flickered in her gaze that surely could not be sadness, Santino told himself. Arianna was a beautiful, rich heiress and she wanted for nothing.

'My mother cleared off to the other side of the world with her lover when I was eleven,' she told him in a hard voice. 'My father didn't know how to deal with my "difficult behav-iour" when I cried every night. He was so des-perate to send me back to boarding school that he drove me there himself—the first and last time he took any interest in my education. I didn't see him again for months. Every school holiday, he used to send me out to Villa Ca-denza with a nanny.'

She snatched her sunglasses out of Santino's fingers and replaced them on her nose. 'The only thing I learned from my parents is to put *me* first, and look after myself, because no one else gives a damn.'

CHAPTER THREE

ARIANNA WISHED SHE could speak Italian better as she tried to explain to the receptionist in the beauty salon that, if the tall man who was standing in the street came into the salon and asked for her, she was to tell him that Miss Fitzgerald was having her legs waxed in one of the treatment rooms.

'You have *appuntamento*?' the girl asked, studying the appointments book on her desk.

'No.' Arianna opened her purse and took out a wad of notes. 'I haven't booked any treatments. I just want you to pretend to the man outside that I will be here in the salon for a few hours—*per favore*,' she added, remembering Santino's jibe about her manners.

She handed the confused-looking receptionist the money before she walked to the back of the building and exited into a small courtyard that she had discovered by chance on a previous visit to the salon. A door at the rear of the building adjacent to the beauty salon led to a flight of stairs, and at the top she entered a large workroom. There were several tables with sewing machines and around the room were tailor's dummies draped with material.

'So you are here at last. But you are late.' The woman who greeted Arianna was small and round, with jet-black hair swept into a severe bun and fierce black eyes. 'If you want to learn to sew from the best seamstress on the Amalfi coast, I expect you to be here at the time we arranged.'

'I'm sorry...*mi dispiace*,' Arianna said meekly.

Rosa handed her a length of muslin. 'Probably you have forgotten everything I taught you last summer, but we will see. You can begin by showing me that you can construct a French seam.'

Arianna nodded and immediately set to work. For years she had fought against the idea of becoming a fashion designer. She had been determined to distance herself from her father, not follow in his footsteps. But a year ago she had acknowledged that ignoring her creativity was making her unhappy. She had a natural flare for designing and sketching clothes, and she loved playing around with different materials, textures and colours. She knew instinctively when an outfit looked right or wrong, the importance of how a material draped and the need for precision tailoring to create a truly beautiful garment.

Last summer while she'd been staying in Positano she had commissioned an evening gown from local designer and dressmaker Rosa Cucinotta. Rosa had shown her around her workroom and it had been a defining moment for Arianna, confirming her decision that she wanted a career in fashion design. But although she had good drawing skills she needed to learn how to sew, make patterns and know how to construct a garment.

She had dismissed the idea of applying to study fashion design at a college in England for fear that the press would find out. It was important to keep her hope of one day owning her own fashion label a secret, especially from her father. If she did make a successful career, she wanted it to be on her own, without Randolph's money or influence.

She had persuaded Rosa to give her sewing lessons, and when she'd returned to London last autumn she had studied with Sylvia Harding, a famous fashion designer who, before she'd retired, had been a couturier to royalty. During the six months that Arianna had spent in Australia, she had worked with a couple of funky young designers in Sydney. For the first time in her life she had had to work hard, and she'd loved it.

For the next hour she concentrated on pinning and cutting the material, before using a sewing machine to make a neat seam that she hoped would be up to Rosa's high standards. Finally she looked up, feeling reasonably happy with her efforts. She was sitting next to the window that overlooked the street and had a perfect view of Santino seated at a table outside the café opposite the dress shop and the beauty salon next door.

The constant presence of a bodyguard following her around was going to make it difficult to spend a few hours every day at Rosa's workshop, she thought with a frown. It would be easier if she told Santino that she was having sewing lessons, but she was reluctant to reveal her dream of establishing her own fashion label.

Her stomach squirmed with shame as she remembered how he had called her a leech who relied on her father for money. At the age of twenty-five she knew she should be independent, although many of her peers in her social circle—the offspring of super-rich parents—lived off trust funds and vast inheritances. But she wanted to be her own person—whoever that was, Arianna thought wryly. She had spent her teenage years and early twenties hating her father, but the result was that she'd become someone she did not like or respect.

As she stared at Santino she felt that strange breathless sensation that only he had ever induced in her. His long legs were stretched out in front of him and his impressive biceps showed beneath his short-sleeved T-shirt. She had noticed earlier that he had a tattoo of a snarling tiger on his upper right arm. He glanced at his watch. No doubt he was bored waiting for her but he would have to get used to it. It occurred to Arianna that she would not need to fire Santino—all she had to do was behave so badly that he was bound to resign from his post as her bodyguard.

'Are you sewing or admiring the scenery?' Rosa asked drily.

Arianna quickly jerked her head round and felt her face grow warm when the dressmaker moved closer to the window and looked at Santino. 'Is he your lover?'

'No! Definitely not.'

'A pity.' Rosa shrugged her ample shoulders. 'He is very handsome.' She picked up the length of fabric that Arianna had been working on and inspected the neat seam. '*Eccellente.* You have improved a lot since last summer when you began sewing lessons with me. You still have much to learn, of course, but I can see you have a natural skill.'

'Thank you.' Arianna blushed again. She was not used to being praised, which was partly her own fault, she acknowledged. As a child she had sought attention from her various nannies by misbehaving, and she'd done the same with her father. At least when Randolph had been angry with her it meant that he'd actually noticed her. But mostly her father had treated her with crucifying indifference on the rare occasions when they met. He travelled extensively for his work, and Arianna had felt the same sense of abandonment that had been so devastating when her mother had left her behind to start a new life in Australia.

Meeting Celine in Sydney after they had not seen each other for more than a decade had been a strange experience, Arianna mused. She had been shocked to discover that she had a half-brother, Jason, who was nearly fifteen. Her mother had explained that she'd been pregnant by her Australian lover when she'd left her husband and daughter. She had wanted to take Arianna to Australia with her, but Randolph had refused to allow it, and he had offered Celine a large amount of money in return for her agreement not to seek custody of Arianna or contact her.

Celine had sacrificed a relationship with her daughter and accepted the pay-off from Randolph, which had allowed her to bring up her son. Arianna understood her mother's reasons but it hadn't hurt any less to hear that she had been used as a pawn in her parents' bitter divorce.

At least she was back in touch with Celine and, although they would never have a close mother-daughter bond, Arianna had promised to visit her mum in Australia and get to know her stepbrother. She was about to start a new chapter in her life and launch her career. For the first time ever she had a sense of purpose and she had surprised herself with her fierce determination to succeed as a designer.

Her unexpected fascination with Santino Vasari was as annoying as it was inexplicable. Once again, Arianna's gaze was drawn to the window, and as she stared at Santino she unconsciously traced her tongue over her lips where his mouth had branded hers. She could still taste him, and she could remember in vivid detail the hunger in his kiss—the glorious, blazing heat of it that had burned through her and pooled, molten and yearning, low in her pelvis.

It made no sense that she was attracted to one of her father's minions. She was certain that Santino had been hired by Randolph to police her behaviour and she didn't understand why she was tempted to tell him that most of the stories about her had been fabricated by the paparazzi. She had pretended to be a social butterfly, aimlessly flitting from one glamorous party to another and from one celebrity lover to another, to punish her father and remind him of her existence.

But admitting those things would be akin to ripping away the mask she had hidden behind the whole of her adult life to reveal the real Arianna Fitzgerald—the vulnerable, un-confident woman...the lonely girl who expected everyone to let her down. She could not be side-tracked by a man who said he was her protector but who, her instincts warned, was dangerous to her peace of mind. She was just starting out on a journey of self-discovery and she was not ready to deal with the disturbing effect that her bodyguard had on her. Deep down, she suspected that she would never be ready for Santino Vasari's devastating sensuality.

* * *

'I swear your nail polish is the same colour it was before you went into the beauty salon two hours ago,' Santino said tersely when Arianna walked over to where he was sitting outside the café.

He stood up as she approached and she had to tilt her head to look at his face. She hated that she felt small and ridiculously fragile when he towered over her. He was easily several inches over six feet tall, but more than his impressively muscular physique he exuded a latent power and an air of command that she guessed came from his time in the army.

She dropped her phone into her bag and gave a careless shrug. 'They're acrylics and need to be replaced every two weeks. I did warn you that you would get bored,' she murmured with a saccharine-sweet smile that evidently did nothing to lighten his black mood.

His heavy brows drew together. 'Seriously, can't you think of anything more interesting to do than spending hours having your body pampered?'

'Seriously, you need to remember that you

are an employee, and not my spiritual guide whose job is to lead me towards enlightenment and a better life,' Arianna told him furiously. She spun round and marched along the street, straight past where her car was parked. 'I've just had a call from my friend Jonny, inviting me to spend the afternoon on his yacht. I won't require a bodyguard,' she said to Santino over her shoulder. 'You might as well go back to the villa and I'll call you later this evening when I want you to collect me.'

She increased her pace and walked swiftly through the pedestrianised streets, past pretty restaurants, art galleries and clothes shops with brightly coloured dresses displayed on rails outside. In midsummer Positano was full of tourists and she had to weave her way through the crowds on the steps down to the beach. She had almost reached Giovanni's' Bar when she sensed someone close behind her, and she turned her head and glared at Santino.

'Go away,' she hissed. 'I can't enjoy a drink with my friends when you are hanging around. I don't want to admit that you are my...' She had been about to say 'minder', but he interrupted her.

'Babysitter,' Santino mocked. 'Don't worry, I'll be discreet,' he drawled as he followed her into the bar.

Most of the crowd who Arianna had met the previous day were in the bar and she joined Davina Huxley-Brown at a table and ordered a drink. What she really wanted to do was go back to Villa Cadenza and work on her designs. But it was Filippo and Ida's afternoon off. She'd felt uncomfortable at the prospect of being alone with Santino at the villa, which was why she had accepted Jonny's invitation.

'Jonny is sending the motor launch over to collect us,' Davina told her. 'Who's the hunk that you arrived with?'

Arianna pretended to be puzzled. 'I didn't arrive with anyone.'

'Shame. I was hoping you could introduce me to the gorgeous guy over there.'

Arianna followed her friend's gaze across the bar and saw Santino chatting to the Dutch twins Poppy and Posy Van Deesen. He was about as discreet as a nuclear explosion, she thought, gritting her teeth when she watched him flirting with the two attractive blondes. Of course he had to glance over in her direction at that exact moment and caught her staring at him. Hot-faced, she turned her head away and took a gulp of her gin and tonic before she remembered that she hadn't eaten breakfast or lunch.

The launch drew up alongside the wooden jetty on the beach and Arianna and some of the others climbed aboard. She immediately put on a life-jacket, although most people did not bother. Minutes later the dingy was zipping over the sparkling sea to where the luxury motor yacht *Sun Princess* was anchored some way off shore.

'You look better than you did yesterday.' Jonny greeted her when she boarded the yacht. He beckoned to a steward who stepped forward and handed her a glass of champagne. It would be churlish to refuse, but she definitely did not need any more alcohol, Arianna decided as she strolled along the deck, looking for somewhere to put down her drink. She felt an odd sensation that she was being watched, and when she glanced over her shoulder she saw that the steward was staring at her. For some reason a shiver ran through her. She did not remember seeing that particular steward on board the yacht yesterday, but she'd been so jet-lagged that most of the day was a blur.

She whirled round at the sound of a familiar voice, and anger fizzed inside her when she saw Santino step onto the deck of the yacht, followed by the Van Deesen twins. The launch had returned to pick up the remaining guests from the beach and bring them out to the *Sun Princess*, and evidently he had managed to get himself included. Poppy Van Deesen linked her arm though his and her twin sister clung to his other arm.

'This is Santino,' Poppy announced. 'He was all alone in the bar, so we asked him if he would like to hang out with us. I hope no one objects?'

'No objection from me,' Davina murmured. 'I'll be happy to hang out with him any day. She looked at Arianna. 'You are rather overdressed, darling. Aren't you going to get changed?'

'I forgot to bring a bikini with me.' Arianna had not planned to spend the afternoon on the yacht and she was feeling hot and uncomfortable in her skinny jeans.

'I have a spare you can borrow.' Davina fished into her bag and pulled out a turquoise bikini. 'You're bigger up top than me so the cup size may be a bit small.' She shrugged. 'But it might mean you get noticed by our sexy new guest.'

Attracting Santino's attention was the last thing she wanted to do, Arianna thought darkly when she returned to the deck wearing the borrowed bikini. The top was strapless and she was scared to move in case her breasts spilled out. She looked across the deck and saw him surrounded by a group of girls, including the twins and Davina.

Following her out to the yacht was taking his bodyguard duties too far. But his real job and the reason her father had hired Santino was to make sure she stayed out of the newspaper headlines, she reminded herself. She lay back on a sun lounger and flicked through a magazine but it was difficult to ignore Santino's sexy, accented voice mingled with the high-pitched laughter of the girls who flocked around him.

Evidently he was too busy enjoying himself to take any notice of her. Arianna felt a hot rush of jealousy that made her furious with herself. She was no longer that person who needed to be the centre of attention. She'd grown up and taken charge of her life, or at least she had made a start. Santino made her revert to the old Arianna, the person she hadn't liked, the person she had vowed never to be again.

Cursing beneath her breath, she jumped up and walked along the deck away from Santino and his fan club of adoring females. At the stern of the yacht she saw Hugo Galbraith, whom she had dated briefly, about to take one of the jet-skis out.

'Hop on,' he called to her. 'I'll take you for a ride.'

Arianna glanced over her shoulder and saw Posy Van Deesen perch herself on Santino's knees. The Dutch beauty was all over him like a rash. Not that Santino seemed to mind, she thought irritably. On impulse she grabbed a life-jacket and stepped down to the docking platform so that she could climb onto the jet-ski. She sat behind Hugo, but as she fastened the straps on the life-jacket she realised that it was too big. Hugo had already started the engine and he opened the throttle to send the jet-ski skimming over the sea.

'Go back,' she shouted, but the jet-ski was moving fast and her words were whipped away on the breeze. She held on tightly around Hugo's waist, hoping he would make it a short trip. They were already a good way away from the *Sun Princess.* Personal watercraft were not allowed close to the beach but this far out from the shore there were a few jet-skis and speed boats racing around.

Arianna suddenly saw a jet-ski moving rapidly over the water heading towards them. She tapped Hugo's shoulder to alert him to the danger and he pulled the handlebars round to turn their jet-ski in a different direction. But they were moving too fast to make such a sharp turn. Everything happened so quickly that Arianna barely had time to cry out as she and Hugo were thrown off the jet-ski.

The shock of landing in the cold sea made her gasp, and she choked as she took a mouthful of water. The ill-fitting life-jacket did not support her properly and her face was partially submerged. A little way off the riderless jet-ski was still hurtling round in circles, causing a whirlpool effect that was dragging Arianna under. She realised that Hugo must not have attached the kill cord which would have stopped the jet-ski's engine when he had been thrown off.

Terrified, she gasped for breath and her mouth filled with water again as waves created by the out-of-control jet-ski crashed over her head. Memories of when she had almost drowned as a child flashed into her mind and she thrashed her arms and kicked her legs to try to keep afloat.

The other jet-ski that moments ago had been racing across the water now slowed down and came up close to Arianna.

'*Signorina!*'

The rider held out his hand, indicating that

he would pull her onto his jet-ski. But she could not move and she felt numb with shock and fear as her face slipped beneath the surface again and her nostrils filled with water.

'Arianna, hang on. I'm coming for you.'

Startled to hear a familiar, commanding voice, she turned her head and saw Santino in the motor launch that was being driven by one of the yacht's crewmen.

'*Signorina*, take my hand.'

The stranger on the jet-ski leaned down and tried to grab hold of Arianna's shoulder. She heard a splash, and when she looked back at the launch she saw that Santino had dived in to the sea and was swimming towards her. In a matter of seconds he was beside her and wrapped his arms around her, lifting her up so that her face was out of the water.

'I've got you, baby.'

His voice was oddly rough, almost as if he was concerned for her, as if he cared—which obviously was a figment of her imagination, Arianna told herself. But she curled her arms around his neck and clung to him, weak with relief that her life was not going to end at the bottom of the ocean. She was vaguely aware that the stranger on the jet-ski turned his craft around and raced away. Santino hooked his arm around her beneath her breasts and towed her to the launch where the crewman helped to pull her on board.

Reaction set in and she hugged her arms around her and fought off a surge of nausea. Santino had climbed back onto the boat, and he draped a towel around her shoulders. He hunkered down in front of her, and even in her shocked state she noticed that he had stripped off his jeans and T-shirt before he'd dived in to the sea and his wet boxer shorts clung to his hips.

'Next time, make sure you wear a life-vest that fits,' he growled.

Arianna couldn't stop shivering. 'Where's Hugo?' she asked through her chattering teeth.

'Another crewman managed to jump from the launch onto the jet-ski and take control of it before he picked your boyfriend up.' Santino frowned as a shudder ran through her. He lifted his hand and smoothed her wet hair back from her face. 'You had a bad scare, but you're safe now, *piccola.*'

The gentle endearment—she knew that the English translation was 'little one'—was her undoing. She had been so afraid, and without Santino's quick actions it was very likely that she would have drowned. Arianna bit down hard on her lip but her emotions overwhelmed her and she burst into tears. 'I thought I was going to drown,' she choked. 'The life-jacket didn't keep me afloat and I can't swim.'

Santino swore as he put his arms around her and pulled her close. His wet chest hairs felt soft beneath Arianna's cheek and the powerful thud of his heart reverberated through her. She heard him speaking in Italian and was aware that the launch was moving, but even though she was safe she couldn't forget those terrifying moments when her mouth had filled with sea water. She wanted to be able to shrug off what had happened as another stupid scrape that she had a reputation for getting herself into. But she couldn't pull herself together and she pressed her face into Santino's chest to muffle her sobs.

CHAPTER FOUR

SANTINO WAS NOT good with tears. They made him uncomfortable and reminded him too much of when his mother had died and his father had wept like a child. Antonio Vasari's outpouring of raw emotion had seemed shameful to his fifteen-year-old son. Santino had not known how to cope with the stranger his father had become.

The once strong, cheerful man whom Santino had idolised had been destroyed by grief as surely as Santino's mother's life had been destroyed by an aggressive brain tumour. The specialist had given Dawn Vasari a year to live, but she'd lasted barely six months, leaving behind a heartbroken husband, teenage son and eight-year-old daughter.

Santino had begged his father to take the family back to Sicily, from where they had moved to Devon a year before his mother's illness had been diagnosed. But Antonio had refused to leave the place where his wife had been born and had died unfairly young. Santino's memories of his late teens were of roaming over desolate Dartmoor for hours, often days, at a time, trying to make sense of life and loss and the realisation that *love* was not worth the agony.

He had cried on the day of his mother's funeral, alone in his bedroom, while his father and sister and his mother's relatives had been downstairs, united somehow in their grief. But he'd felt like an outsider and he hadn't wanted their sympathy. He'd wanted to punch something. His tears had not helped to ease the pain in his heart and he hadn't cried again. Ever.

He understood fear. He'd seen it in the eyes of some of the men from his patrol in Afghanistan when they had been ambushed and for a while it had looked as if none of them would survive. He knew what it was like to look death in the face. He tightened his arms around Arianna's trembling body and let her cry it out.

Grimly he acknowledged that he had failed

to protect her. He'd jumped into the launch as soon as he'd seen her on the back of the jet-ski, and witnessing the accident when she'd been thrown into the sea had caused his heart to miss a beat. He frowned as he recalled the dangerous behaviour of the other jet-skier. The rider had appeared deliberately to drive towards the craft that Arianna and her friend had been on. It was almost as if he'd wanted to cause an accident. And then he'd tried to pull Arianna onto his jet-ski. Had the jet-skier wanted to rescue her, or had there been something more sinister behind his actions?

Santino ran his hand around the back of his neck and over his scar. The kidnappers must be aware that Arianna was in Positano after she'd appeared on the front page of the newspapers. But how could they have known that she had gone out on the jet-ski unless they had been close by—perhaps on one of the other yachts anchored in the bay—and had been watching her through binoculars? The incident with the jet-skis was probably nothing to worry about, he tried to reassure himself. But his instincts warned him that the threat to Arianna was very real.

The launch stopped in the shallows close to a small, secluded beach that was not often discovered by tourists. As Santino had hoped, it was empty. After giving instructions to the crewman, he scooped Arianna into his arms and carried her up the beach, depositing her carefully on the sand and dropping down onto his knees beside her.

'Lie back while I check you over,' he ordered after he'd helped her out of the life-jacket. To his surprise she did not argue. 'Are you hurt anywhere? Your body took quite an impact when you came off the jet-ski at speed and hit the water.'

'I'm okay.' Her eyes were closed and she spoke so softly that he had to lean closer to hear her. 'I'm just shaken up.'

'I'm not surprised.' He felt a knot of tension in his gut when he thought of how easily she could have drowned if he hadn't reached her in time.

Her lashes flew open and he stared into her big brown eyes, watching the golden flecks on her irises reflect the gleam from the sun in the cobalt-blue sky above them. She was so god damned beautiful. He pushed the thought away, determined to remain professional as he ran his hands over her arms and down her legs, checking for any broken bones.

'Why did you go on the jet-ski if you can't swim?'

'Because I'm an idiot. That's what you think, isn't it?' she said flatly. 'It's the opinion my father has of me—when he thinks of me at all, which isn't very often.'

Santino didn't know what to make of this different Arianna with hurt in her voice and that air of vulnerability that he'd assumed was an act when they had been at the Villa Cadenza. He'd felt certain that he had her measure. Spoilt and privileged with little of substance beneath her exquisite packaging. He frowned as he remembered that he'd found Randolph Fitzgerald a cold and arrogant man when he had met him.

'I don't think you are an idiot,' he said roughly. 'How come you never learned to swim when there's that amazing pool at Villa Cadenza?'

'I nearly drowned when I was a young child. I must have only been three or four and the incident left me with a fear of being out of my depth in water.' Catching his questioning look, she explained, 'I was with my parents at a hotel somewhere. I don't remember where. My father travels around the world for his business, and before my parents' marriage broke up my mother and I occasionally went with him.

'On the day that it happened my father had taken me to play in the shallow part of the pool. But while he was talking on his phone I must have waded deeper. I was terrified when I realised that I couldn't feel the floor of the pool beneath my feet. I remember calling to my father, but he was some distance away, and because he was on his phone he didn't hear me.'

Arianna sat up and hugged her knees to her chest. 'I remember the sensation of my mouth filling with water. I was choking and couldn't breathe. Luckily another hotel guest arrived at the pool and jumped in and saved me from drowning. When my father finally finished his phone call, he told me off for misbehaving.' She gave a humourless laugh. 'I learned two valuable lessons that day. The first to be fearful of deep water, and the second that my father has little interest in me.'

'It's true that a traumatic event in childhood or teenage years can affect people in their adult lives,' Santino said, remembering the anger that had eaten away at him for a long time after his mother's death. Joining the army had given him a sense of belonging and purpose and he'd learned to deal with his anger. But fighting in a brutal war that had cost the lives of a couple of his close friends had reinforced his wariness—he refused to call it fear—of emotional attachments.

'I tried hypnotism once to try to get over my fear of drowning, but I panic when my face is in the water,' Arianna admitted. 'When my father sent me out of his way to Villa Cadenza every summer, a few of my nannies tried to teach me to swim, but I made such a fuss that they gave up.'

'In future I suggest that you don't allow your boyfriend to take you for a ride on a jet-ski,' Santino growled. He could not understand why, when he had seen Arianna climb onto the jet-ski and wrap her arms around the fair-haired Englishman, he'd felt as though he'd been punched in his stomach. The feeling could not have been jealousy, he assured himself, because no woman had ever evoked that emotion in him—or indeed any emotion other than sexual desire.

Arianna sent him a quick glance. 'Hugo isn't my boyfriend.'

'Your friend Lady Davina something-or-other told me that you're involved with this Hugo guy.'

'She probably said it because she fancies you and wanted to take me out of the competition.' Arianna gave one of those maddeningly nonchalant shrugs that, for reasons he was unable to explain, Santino found infuriating. 'But Davina needn't have worried. I'm not interested in you.'

'No?' The word hung in the hot summer's afternoon air, an unintentional challenge—or maybe not unintentional, Santino acknowledged self-derisively as his eyes locked with Arianna's. Adrenalin was still pumping through him after rescuing her from the sea, and his relief had been mixed with an indefinable emotion when she'd wept in his arms.

Tears still clung to her lashes, but he watched her eyes darken, the pupils dilating. Sexual tension had simmered between them by the pool at Villa Cadenza. Santino had taken one look at her and something had shifted deep inside him. He had told himself it was lust, for how could it be anything else, anything more?

Here on the secluded beach it was as if only the two of them existed. Like the biblical Adam tempted by Eve's sensual promise, he could not take his eyes from Arianna wearing another sexy bikini that showed off her stunning figure. He was conscious of his heart pounding in his chest and the heat of the sun on his back as he slowly bent his head.

Her breasts rose and fell, and he heard her swiftly indrawn breath, but she did not move— she simply stared at him with her brown eyes lit with gold. She was an irresistible temptation and with a low groan he claimed her mouth with his.

He tasted salt from the sea on her lips and

when he dipped his tongue into her mouth her sweet breath mingled with his. She hesitated for a heartbeat that felt to Santino like a lifetime. With a sense of urgency he had never experienced before he increased the pressure of his lips on hers, and his heart clattered against his ribs when she tipped her head back and opened her mouth to him.

Her surrender shattered the last remnants of his self-control. Santino forgot the rules he had set himself as he deepened the kiss and explored the sensual shape of her lips before he delved into her mouth and tangled his tongue with hers. It was hot and intense. He was blown away by Arianna's passionate response as he felt a shudder run through her when he trailed his lips over her cheek and gently nipped her ear lobe with his teeth.

He kissed his way down her elegant neck and along the fragile line of her collar bone. Her skin was like satin and her breasts felt soft against the hard wall of his chest when he slid his arms around her and pulled her into his heat. She moved her hands up to his shoulders and he eased her down onto the sand, stretching out beside her so that he could skim his fingertips over the tantalising dips and curves of her body.

Her narrow waist fascinated him, the gentle flare of her hips even more so. He was so hard it hurt. He thought he might explode if he did not have her, if he did not sink between her silken thighs and drive his shaft home. The feminine scent of her arousal was the sweetest fragrance and he was certain that her hunger was as intense his. Her breathing was as unsteady as the erratic thud of his heart.

Driven by a need greater than he had ever known, Santino traced his fingers over Arianna's skimpy bikini pants that sat low on her hips. He felt her stomach quiver but, when he slipped his hand between her legs, she tensed.

'No.'

The word detonated inside his head and catapulted him back to reality. *What the hell was he doing?* He could not make love to Arianna. Love played no part in what he wanted, Santino acknowledged. He was desperate to have sex with her, but he must not give in to the desire that ran hot and wild in his veins. He was appalled by his lack of finesse. He'd behaved like a hormone-fuelled teenager and almost lost his self-control. It had never happened before and he was rocked by the effect that Arianna had on him.

He levered himself so that he was sitting upright and lifted his hand to shield his eyes from the glare of the sun while he scanned the empty beach. It was his job to protect her, but if the kidnappers arrived at the secluded bay he would stand little chance of keeping her safe from a ruthless and probably armed gang.

Arianna sat up and ran her fingers through her hair that was drying into tangled curls around her shoulders and made her look younger than did her usual sleek style. Her eyes were huge and dark in her delicate face. Santino dragged his gaze from her pert breasts half-spilling out of her bikini top. 'I guess this is not the time or the place,' he muttered.

Her eyes flashed fire at him. 'You guess right. There isn't a time or a place when I would agree to have casual sex with you.'

Stung by her snippy tone, he said curtly, 'That's not the impression you gave a few moments ago. You wanted me.' His eyes narrowed. 'Or is that the kind of game you like to play? There is a word for women who deliberately lead men on.'

'Are you saying that I'm not allowed to change my mind?' Her voice was sharp, but Santino noticed that her mouth trembled and something tugged in his chest. 'I admit I got carried away, but I hadn't expected you to kiss me.' She looked around the secluded beach and back to him, biting her lip. 'Why did you bring me here instead of taking me back to the yacht? And why did you send the launch away?' Her tension was tangible. 'Did you intend to seduce me? Maybe you think I owe you for rescuing me?'

'Of course I don't think that,' he denied roughly. 'You were in an emotional state after the incident with the jet-ski and I thought you might want some time to pull yourself together before we returned to the yacht.'

Santino's jaw clenched as shame rolled through him. He prided himself on his integrity but Arianna's accusation had hit a mark. She had been traumatised after being thrown off the jet-ski and the accident had brought back memories of how she had nearly drowned as a child. Once again he had been struck by her vulnerability, but that had not stopped him coming on to her. His body still ached to possess her and with a curse he jumped up and ran down the beach, diving into the waves and striking powerfully through the water.

A few minutes later he heard a boat's engine and saw the launch returning to the little cove. It ran up onto the sand and he waded through the shallows and spoke to the crewman. When he looked back up the beach, he couldn't see Arianna, and fear gripped him. It would be impossible for the kidnappers to have snatched her in the few minutes that he hadn't been with her, he told himself.

To his relief he spotted her over by some rocks, but as he walked towards her she backed away from him. 'I can't face going on the launch.' She hugged her arms around her body and her mouth crumpled. 'I know you must think I'm stupid.'

He frowned. 'Why do you put yourself down?' For reasons he could not explain to himself, Santino wanted to take her in his arms and comfort her as he had done after she'd been thrown off the jet-ski. 'Your fear of drowning is perfectly understandable after your childhood experience. I don't think you are an idiot, or stupid.'

Santino had a suspicion that Arianna was far more astute than she allowed people to think, but now was not the time to wonder why she played to the tabloids' opinion of her as an empty-headed socialite. He held out her bag containing her clothes. 'I sent the crewman back to the yacht to collect your things. Get dressed. We can return to the town via the stairs that climb up the cliff from the beach.'

She stared at him with wide, wary eyes, but then she suddenly smiled. Not the carefully choreographed smile he'd noticed she kept pinned to her face when she had been with her jet-set friends aboard the yacht. The smile she gave him was spontaneous and warm, and it stole his breath. 'Thank you,' she said softly.

There were three hundred steps winding up the steep cliff. Santino counted every one of them in an attempt to keep his mind and his gaze from Arianna's sexy derriere covered in tight-fitting, white denim jeans. They walked back to the car in silence and she didn't argue when he slid behind the wheel. Earlier he had called Filippo and arranged for someone to collect the four-by-four.

On the way back to the villa he glanced at Arianna and saw that she had fallen asleep. No doubt she was still shocked by the accident with the jet-ski, he thought grimly. The breeze blew strands of her chestnut-brown hair across her face. He recalled those moments on the beach when her body had trembled beneath his touch and his jaw tightened as he forced his gaze back to the road.

Fifteen minutes later he parked in the courtyard at the front of Villa Cadenza and touched her shoulder. 'Wake up, Sleeping Beauty.'

Her long lashes swept upwards and she regarded him sleepily with her velvet brown eyes. Santino could not bring himself to look away from her, from her mouth that was a sensual temptation even before she ran her tongue over her bottom lip. And the crazy thing was his feeling that it had been a wholly unconscious invitation, as if she was unaware of the effect she had on him.

He ran his hand around the back of his neck and felt the scar left by the bullet that had nearly claimed his life. A permanent reminder of the frailty of humankind. 'What happened earlier was a regrettable mistake,' he said curtly. 'I should not have kissed you.'

Her brows rose. 'Aren't all mistakes, by definition, regrettable? And surely you mean two mistakes? You kissed me by the pool this morning and then again on the beach this afternoon,' she reminded him.

'The first kiss was instigated by you.'

'I didn't hear you complain,' she said mildly.

He scowled at her. 'The point I am making,' he growled, 'is that it can't happen again.'

Arianna stepped out of the car and flashed him a brittle smile that made him wonder what had happened to the girl on the beach whose smile had lit up her lovely face, or if she had even existed outside of his imagination.

'You would be more convincing if you

stopped staring at me as if you're visualising me naked in your bed,' she murmured, before she sauntered into the house, leaving Santino with a mental picture of her that instantly made him hard. He clenched his hands on the steering wheel while he fought the temptation to go after her and demonstrate that she was nowhere near as immune to him as she pretended to be.

The discordant sound of voices arguing broke the almost cloistered quiet of the workroom above Rosa's dress shop. Arianna glanced at her watch and was startled to see that she had been engrossed in her work for the past three hours.

After she'd shown Rosa some sketches of a cocktail dress that she had designed, the seamstress had suggested she should make a *toile*— a rough model of the dress made from muslin. Usually the *toile* would be placed on a tailor's dummy to see how the garment draped. But Arianna planned to make the dress for herself out of mulberry silk, and she had tried the *toile* on to check the fit before she worked with an expensive fabric.

She moved away from the mirror to look out of the window at the rear of the workroom and her heart sank when she saw Santino standing in the courtyard below. He was having a heated conversation with the manageress of the beauty salon. Damn the man, Arianna thought as she took off the *toile* and hurriedly pulled on her skirt and top.

At the villa the previous evening she had been furious when she'd discovered that he had confiscated the keys to both of her cars. But her accusation that she was a prisoner in her own home had elicited no sympathy from Santino. 'You can drive either of your vehicles as long as I accompany you to wherever you are going,' he'd told her.

But Arianna doubted that he would fall for her excuse of visiting the beauty salon again while she was actually at Rosa's workroom. Determined that Santino should not find out about her sewing lessons, she had slipped out of Villa Cadenza early in the morning and caught a bus into the town. Using public transport was a novelty that she would need to get used to in the future when she would have to rely on earning her own income from her fashion business.

Santino must have realised that she was missing from the villa and had driven into Positano to search for her. Although her Italian was limited, Arianna gathered that he had accused the manageress of the beauty salon of being involved in her disappearance. As she ran down the staircase from the workroom she fumbled to pull up the zip on her skirt and emerged into the courtyard flushed and breathless. 'What are you doing here?' she asked Santino crossly.

He jerked his head in her direction, and she was shocked by his strained expression. His skin looked grey beneath his tan, and his hair was dishevelled, as if he'd run his fingers through it many times.

'*Arianna.*' He strode over to her. 'Are you all right? I feared—' He broke off abruptly.

She was puzzled. 'You feared what, exactly?'

He did not reply and there was no clue to his thoughts on his chiselled features. She grimaced. 'I suppose you were worried that I was up to no good.'

'Again,' Santino said drily, and the contempt in his voice brought a flush of colour to her cheeks. His eyes narrowed and she had an odd feeling that he wanted to say something else, but at that moment the door behind her banged shut in the breeze.

Santino looked up at the window of the building that she had exited from and frowned. 'Why did you leave the villa without me? I told you, it is your father's wish that I should accompany you whenever you go out.'

'And I told you that I need some privacy. I'm sick of my father's attempts to control my life,' Arianna said bitterly. She stiffened when Santino flicked his hard gaze over her.

'Did you get dressed in a hurry? Your shirt is buttoned up wrong.'

She looked down at her sleeveless cotton shirt and saw that she had misaligned the buttons in the button holes.

'Why all the secrecy?' he demanded. 'The woman in the beauty salon told me that you didn't have your nails done yesterday and you weren't even in the salon. So where did you go?'

He moved towards the door behind Arianna, and she knew that if he opened it he was bound to climb the stairs and discover Rosa's workroom. She stepped in front of him to bar his way, but he was so much bigger than her, and he would easily be able to push past her. With a deep sense of reluctance she decided that she would have to tell him about her sewing lessons.

'I came here to meet someone,' she muttered.

Santino's gaze lingered on her wrongly buttoned shirt before moving up to her hair that had come loose from her chignon. Strands of hair curled around her face. It had been warm in Rosa's workroom, and Arianna could feel that her cheeks were pink. He looked up at the window again. From the outside of the building there was no indication that the room on the second story was a workroom. It could be a private apartment above the shop. Santino watched her fasten her shirt properly and his jaw hardened.

'By "someone" I assume you mean a lover,'

he said harshly. 'Did you get up from his bed and dress in a hurry before you came down to meet me?'

Arianna was so taken aback by his accusation that she said nothing. Santino continued in a clipped voice, 'So, did you spend yesterday afternoon with this guy while I sat outside the damn café, drinking endless cups of coffee, and waited for you?' His green eyes glittered. 'I suppose that's why you sneaked out of the villa today?'

'I did not sneak out.'

Santino had given her a convenient excuse for her trips into Positano and Arianna was under no obligation to tell him the truth. She felt a little pang in her heart, thinking that she must have imagined the gentle concern he had shown her on the beach the previous day. He was constructed of iron and granite and there was no chink in his armour. 'My personal life is my business and I can do whatever I like, with whomever I like,' she told him coolly.

'As your bodyguard, I need to know where you are going and who you are meeting.'

Arianna's temper simmered. He made her feel like a naughty schoolgirl and she was incensed that he would report her every action to her father. Santino was effectively spying on her and she knew why. No doubt Randolph was anxious to avoid a scandal like the one she had been involved in a year ago, when the tabloids had printed graphic details of her alleged wild night of sex with a famous footballer.

The story had been pure fabrication. She'd danced with the footballer at a nightclub and they had been spotted by the paparazzi leaving the venue together. What hadn't been reported was that Scott Hunter had flagged down a taxi for her, and she had returned home alone with a blinding headache that had turned out to be the start of a severe bout of the flu.

She lifted her chin and fixed Santino with an icy glare. 'Do you seriously expect me to give you a list of my lovers?'

'From what I've heard, it's a long list,' he said bitingly.

For a split second it crossed Arianna's mind to tell him that the rumours and gossip about her were untrue. But why would he believe her? It was obvious that he believed the tabloid stories. And why did she care what he thought of her? She didn't, she assured herself.

'Can I assume from your judgemental tone that you are a virgin?' she asked him sweetly. 'You have never had a lover because you are saving yourself until you fall in love and decide to marry the lucky recipient of your affections?' He obviously did not like her sarcasm, and his dark brows drew together in a slashing frown when she continued, 'Or is this a case of double standards? It's fine for you to have any number of sexual partners, but if I do the same thing I must be a whore?'

'This is a pointless conversation,' he said through gritted teeth. 'For the record, I don't have any intention of falling in love, and in my opinion marriage is an outdated institution.' His jaw was rigid and Arianna's heart gave a jolt when she realised that he was struggling to control his temper. Common sense warned her not to antagonise him further, but the hard gleam in his eyes sent a heady rush of adrenalin through her.

'Maybe you're frustrated because you can't have me?' she taunted.

He moved faster than she could blink and caught her by her shoulder, pulling her towards him so that her breasts hit the hard wall of his chest and her breath was expelled from her body. She stared into his eyes and realised too late that she had been a fool to play with fire. The heat of his gaze scorched her and the contemptuous curl of his mouth hurt her more than it should.

'We both know that I could have you any time I wanted,' he bit out.

She opened her mouth to deny his arrogant claim, but the words were trapped in her throat. His face was so close to hers that the stubble on his jaw scraped her cheek. His warm breath grazed her lips and a quiver of desire ran like molten fire through her as she tilted her head in readiness for his mouth to claim hers. She was unaware of how utterly she betrayed herself. Her entire being was focused on Santino, on her need for him to kiss her, and she stared at him with wide-eyed incomprehension when he muttered something in Italian and thrust her away from him.

'Somehow the thought that you have come straight from another man's bed lessens your appeal. It's like turning up late to a feast and finding only pickings left,' he drawled. But Arianna sensed from his harsh inhalation of breath that it had cost him to speak in that dismissive manner.

She was tempted to take him upstairs to Rosa's workroom to prove that he was wrong about her—that there was no mystery lover—and she would enjoy watching him grovel. The satisfactory scene that unfolded in her imagination was spoiled by the realisation that, if she revealed to Santino her plans to establish her own fashion label, he was likely to tell her father.

So she gave an airy shrug of her shoulders and put her hand on the door that led to the stairs to the workroom. 'You seem to be under the misapprehension that I care what you think about me, Santino. But here's a news flash—I don't give a damn.' She opened the door and threw him a haughty glance over her shoulder. 'I'll be busy here for another hour and you can wait for me in the car.'

CHAPTER FIVE

IT WAS ONLY because the party was for Jonny's birthday that Arianna decided to attend. Jonny was a good friend, and there were few enough people who she considered to be true and trustworthy friends, she acknowledged ruefully. Having a billionaire for a father meant that she'd had to learn to spot hangers-on and those so-called friends who hoped that an association with her would boost their career or their bank balance. A few times she had been burned, and she would be the first to admit that she had an issue with trust.

The party was a black-tie event taking place at the hottest nightclub on the Amalfi coast. Indira Club was in Amalfi town, along the coast from Positano, and the venue had been hired out exclusively for the party. The guest list was a mix of the great and good—wealthy socialites from across Europe and A-list celebrities who Jonny knew from his reality television show, *Toffs*. It was inevitable that the paparazzi would be present outside the club in droves— the pap pack hunting the brat pack with their long-lens cameras.

Arianna had made the decision a year ago to step away from the glitzy world she had been part of since she was eighteen. Her brush with death when a bout of the flu had developed into a serious case of pneumonia had led to her re-evaluating her life. It was ironic, she mused, that the best way to get her designs noticed when she launched her fashion company would be to grab the media's attention any way she could. But establishing her own fashion label was not a whim. She was serious about starting her business, and she had to hope that if the clothes she designed were good enough they would speak for themselves.

The dress she had chosen to wear to the party was one of her own creations. Made of gold silk organza with a tulle overlay, the ball gown had a tight-fitting bodice with narrow shoulder straps and a full skirt. The design was unashamedly romantic and had been inspired by stories of fairy-tale princesses from Arianna's childhood.

All she needed was a handsome prince, she thought wryly as she dabbed perfume on the pulse points at her wrists and neck. She loved the exclusive fragrance that had been created for her by a famous Parisian perfumer, but she would no longer be able to afford bespoke perfume when she launched her fashion business. It would be a small price to pay for her independence from her father though.

Buoyed by that thought, Arianna collected her evening bag and pashmina and headed out of her bedroom. Halfway down the villa's sweeping staircase she saw Santino walk across the entrance hall and her footsteps faltered. He halted at the bottom of the stairs and seemed riveted by her appearance.

'You look exquisite,' he said thickly.

'Thank you.' She tried to sound cool and composed but her voice was annoyingly husky, and she felt herself blush beneath his intense scrutiny as she descended the last few steps. His green eyes gleamed and she glimpsed a feral hunger in his gaze that felt like a kick low in her belly.

He looked incredible in a tuxedo, white silk shirt and black bow tie. The stubble on his jaw had been trimmed and his dark-as-night hair was tidier than usual but still curled rebelliously over his collar.

'Don't you think you are rather overdressed for a bodyguard-cum-chauffeur?' she murmured, feeling a stab of jealousy as she wondered if he intended to meet a woman in Amalfi once he had delivered her to the party.

'The invitation states black tie.' Santino took a gold-edged card out of his jacket pocket. 'Your friend Jonny invited me to the party when I met him on his yacht, after I explained that you and I are *very* good friends.' The suggestive wink he gave infuriated her even more.

'Why on earth did you tell him that?'

'I thought you might prefer that the other guests tonight don't realise I am your bodyguard.'

She glared at him. 'I told you, there is no need for you to be at the Indira Club. The party is invitation only and the paparazzi will be prevented from entering the club. If you must, you can escort me to the door to make sure I don't do anything outrageous that would guarantee my photograph appearing on the front of tomorrow's tabloids.'

'But this—' Santino waved the invitation in front of her '—means that I can attend the party with you. Rather than you having to explain to your friends that I am your minder, it makes sense if I pretend to be your date.'

She shook her head fiercely and her hair, which she'd allowed to dry into its natural, loose, silky curls, bounced on her shoulders. 'No way.'

'You can explain to anyone who asks that we got together after I rescued you when you came off the jet-ski,' Santino continued smoothly, as if she hadn't spoken.

Arianna opened her mouth to tell him that she would rather go to the party with Jack the Ripper than with him. Except that it wasn't true. The glitter in Santino's green eyes intrigued and excited her, and when he offered her his arm she hesitated before she placed her hand on his forearm. Beneath the sleeve of his jacket she felt the latent strength of sinews and muscles. His snarling tiger tattoo was hidden beneath his clothes but Santino was a dangerous beast and she must not forget it.

Tonight, however, the tiger was at least giving the appearance of being tamed. Santino escorted her outside and held the car door open while she climbed in and layers of gold tulle frothed around her. 'Would you like the sun roof open or closed?'

She grimaced. 'Closed, please, or my hair will look like I've been dragged through a hedge.'

'I doubt you could ever look anything other than perfect.'

Arianna glanced at him when he slid into the driver's seat, startled by the deep timbre of his voice. His eyes met hers and that feeling between them that she dared not examine too closely pulsed hard and hot. She swallowed and turned her head to stare out of the window.

'I'm sure Davina will be delighted to see you again, as will Poppy and Posy—the very attractive blonde twins you flirted with on Jonny's yacht,' she reminded him drily when he looked bemused.

'There is no need to be jealous, *cara*. I will only have eyes for you at the party.'

'I'm not *jealous*.' She jerked her head round to glare at him and felt certain that his lips twitched.

As he drove away from the villa she maintained a dignified silence while she struggled to regain her composure. The powerful sports car ate up the miles and soon they were flying along the Amalfi coast road, full of twists and turns and hairpin bends that Santino negotiated with skilful assurance. The scenery was dramatic, with the cliffs towering above the road on one side and a terrifying drop down to the coast on the other. The sun sinking below the horizon cast pink-and-gold streaks across the sky which were reflected on the dark, glassy sea.

Arianna was too pent up to notice the view. 'I'm not your *cara*,' she muttered, angry with herself for the way her heart had given a jolt at his careless endearment.

She had kept out of his way when they'd returned to the villa after he had found her in Positano and tension had simmered between them. But eventually boredom and loneliness had sent her down to the kitchen. Some of her happiest childhood memories were of when Ida had allowed her to help make bread, or she had sat at the table and watched Filippo, whose hobby was mending watches and clocks.

But when she'd entered the kitchen she had found Santino seated at the table, his long legs stretched out in front of him while he sipped a beer and chatted to the elderly couple. Their conversation was in Italian, and Arianna had felt like an intruder when the three of them had fallen silent. She'd quickly poured herself a glass of fruit juice and left.

It reminded her of when she'd been a teenager, on the rare occasions when she had been at home with her father and had walked into a room where he was entertaining guests. Randolph had never introduced her to his friends or asked her to join them and she had felt like an unwelcome visitor in her own home.

When she'd exited the kitchen and closed the door loudly behind her, she had heard Santino resume talking to Filippo and Ida, and her resentment of him had grown. But her conscience had pointed out that if she'd handled things differently instead of behaving like a spoilt brat he might have invited her to stay.

Silly tears stung Arianna's eyes as she recalled how alone she had felt when she'd returned to her bedroom. The rich princess in her ivory tower. She looked at Santino's tanned hands holding the steering wheel, before moving her gaze up to his strong profile, and asked herself why his opinion of her mattered.

'You have an Italian name and speak the language like a native, so how were you able to serve in the British army if you are Italian?' She gave in to her curiosity about him.

'I have dual nationality. My father was Sicilian and my mother was English. I was born in Sicily and lived there until I was a teenager, when we moved to the south west of England.'

'We?'

'My parents and younger sister, Gina. My mother's family are farmers in Devon. She met my father when she was on holiday in Sicily. Apparently they fell in love at first sight, were married within a month and I was born a year later. Madre had seemed happy living in Sicily. Sometimes I've wondered if she knew she was ill and wanted to go back to the place where she had grown up,' Santino said half-beneath his breath. He glanced at Arianna. 'My mother died from a brain tumour eighteen months after we moved to England.'

'I'm sorry,' she said softly. 'The tragedy must have been even harder for you and your father and sister to bear when you hadn't lived in England for long.'

'Yes.' His voice was devoid of emotion but she noticed that he flexed his fingers around the steering wheel and his knuckles whitened.

'Did your father take you and your sister back to live in Sicily after your mother's death?'

'No, he wanted to remain in Devon to be near to her grave. My father never really recovered from her death, and when he died a few years ago I believe it was a release from his unhappiness.'

'That's sad, but also very poignant that he loved your mother so much.'

'Do you think so?' Santino's jaw clenched.

'My father numbed his grief with whisky and left my English grandparents to more or less bring up my sister. Gina was only eight when our mother died. She is a credit to the grandparents who took good care of her, although it is down to her own hard work that she has a successful career as a senior fashion buyer for a top department store in New York.'

Had that been a dig at her lack of a career? Arianna wondered. Santino's sister must have been affected by the loss of their mother, but at least she'd had other family members to fill the void and give her affection. When Celine had moved to Australia and left Arianna behind, no one had paid her any attention, certainly not her father.

'Did your grandparents take care of you too?'

'They did their best, but I was an angry young man and I don't suppose I was particularly likeable.' Santino braked as he steered around a steep bend. 'I felt like an outsider living in a tiny Devon village and, at school, my odd-sounding name and my accent made me different from the other kids. My grandparents tried to get me interested in their farm but I missed my old life and my friends in Sicily.'

He glanced at Arianna and admitted, 'I hated spending hours every day in a cold milking shed with a bunch of cows.' His rueful grin lit a flame inside her and she smiled back at him.

'What made you decide to join the army?'

'By the time I was seventeen, I'd begun to seriously go off the rails, and I'd been in trouble with the police a couple of times for minor offences. There was an army recruitment day at school, and I signed up, because being a soldier seemed a better option than getting a criminal record.' He was silent for a moment. 'Being in the army made me feel that I belonged somewhere and gave me some self-respect.'

'I understand what it's like to feel lost,' she admitted, wondering as she spoke why she had opened up to him when she had never felt an inclination to do so with anyone else.

He frowned. 'How have you ever felt lost, Arianna? You grew up with immense privilege, you are stunningly beautiful and you have the world at your feet. If you feel lost, you only have yourself to blame,' Santino said harshly. 'You could use your wealth, and the media's fascination with you, to great effect by raising money for charities or bringing awareness to social issues. But instead you do nothing better than drift from one party to another and one meaningless affair to another.'

'Not everything you have read about me in the newspapers is true!' she snapped, stung by his criticism. A lot of rubbish had been printed about her, but she felt a sick sense of shame when she remembered various photos of herself falling out of clubs, and on more than one occasion out of her clothes. There had been a time when getting drunk had been preferable to dealing with her emotions, and she'd sought popularity to prove to herself that she wasn't lonely.

She turned her head away from Santino and a tense silence replaced the camaraderie that had briefly existed between them. They arrived in Amalfi, and out of the car window she saw a crowd of photographers in front of the Indira Club. Instead of stopping outside the entrance, Santino turned up a side road, and minutes later he parked the car in an alleyway at the back of the club.

'It will be best if we enter the building through the back door,' he said in answer to her questioning look.

'To avoid the paparazzi, presumably. Has my father offered to pay you a bonus if you keep me out of the tabloids until after Fitzgerald Design's stock market debut?' she asked sarcastically.

'Arianna...' He seemed about to say something else, but when he put his hand on her arm she shrugged him off.

'Randolph manipulates people. It's all part of his control strategy. I should know, because he has tried to control me all my life,' she told Santino bitterly before she swept past him, gathering up her long skirt in her hands to avoid brushing against a stack of empty beer crates by the back door to the club. She didn't look round to see if he was behind her as she marched through the kitchens, ignoring the startled looks of the staff. The voice of the DJ led her to the main area of the club, where the dance floor was already packed with party guests and she spotted Jonny leaning against the bar.

'I didn't see you arrive,' he said as he handed her a flute of champagne and watched her take several long sips. 'That's vintage Krug that you're knocking back like lemonade, darling.' A faint frown crossed Jonny's pleasant features. 'What's wrong, Arianna?'

'Nothing,' she lied. 'I just needed a drink. Do I get to dance with the birthday boy?'

'Only if you can assure me that your ex-army boyfriend won't rip my legs off,' Jonny said wryly. 'He mentioned while we were on the yacht yesterday that he had served in the forces.'

Arianna followed Jonny's gaze across the room to where Santino was leaning against a pillar and was evidently the focus of interest of a group of women nearby. His height made him easy to pick out, and the brooding expression on his devastatingly handsome face caused her heart to give a jolt. She remembered that her father had said in his text message that Santino had been in the SAS. It would account for the steel core that she sensed ran through him. 'It's not what you think,' she muttered to Jonny.

'Maybe you should let Santino know that, if the hungry way he's looking at you is an indication of what *he's* thinking,' Jonny murmured as he led her onto the dance floor.

For the next few hours Arianna sparkled. She flitted from one dance partner to the next like a golden butterfly, and laughed and flirted and drank too much champagne, just as everyone expected of Arianna Fitzgerald, the party princess. She congratulated herself on not looking over her shoulder for Santino, but a sixth sense told her that he was watching her, and she laughed louder and flirted more outrageously with the men who flocked around her. They seemed young and crass compared to Santino's smouldering sensuality, and her breath rushed from her lungs when he appeared in front of her and smoothly took the place of Hugo Galbraith, with whom she had been dancing.

'My turn, I think you'll find,' he told Hugo. His smile did nothing to disguise his dangerous tone and the Englishman stepped back from Arianna with alacrity. She hardly noticed Hugo walk away as her gaze tangled with Santino's green eyes, glittering with what she belatedly realised was fury. He clamped one arm around her waist and his other hand captured hers and held it against the lapel of his jacket, just as the DJ slowed the tempo and played a haunting ballad that had topped the music charts for weeks. 'You are obviously enjoying yourself,' he growled.

'Why wouldn't I have a good time at the party?' she countered, flashing him a brittle smile. 'Socialising is what I do best, after all.'

She felt the muscles in his arm flex as he pulled her closer so that her cheek was pressed against the soft silk of his shirt, and his shockingly hard arousal nudged the junction between her thighs.

'Is he here? Was he one of the pretty boys I saw you dancing with?'

Startled, her lashes swept upwards. 'Who?'

'Your lover.'

'I don't have a lover.' Too late she remembered Santino's assumption that she'd spent the morning with a man when she had actually been in Rosa's workroom. 'Um...what I mean is, no…he isn't at the party. Would it bother you if he was here?'

'Everything about you bothers me, *cara*.'

His rough voice sent a curl of heat through her. She told herself that she must have imagined he'd sounded possessive, or that the hard gleam in his eyes softened a fraction. But she did not imagine that he dipped his face closer to hers, so close that she was mesmerised by the sensual shape of his mouth as he brought it within a millimetre of her lips.

'You can no doubt feel how bothered I am by you,' he drawled. There might have been a hint of self-derision in his voice, but Arianna was only aware of his potent masculinity when he moved his hand to the small of her back and exerted pressure to bring her pelvis into burning contact with his. Feeling the solid ridge of his erection beneath his trousers elicited a flood of molten heat between her legs.

She shivered in the heat of his fire, but when his warm breath grazed her lips she whispered, 'You said you couldn't kiss me again.'

'I lied,' he muttered. And then he proved it by covering her mouth with his.

It was wild and hot. Santino's lips moved over hers with devastating assurance, sipping her, tasting her, and she trembled at the onslaught of his fierce passion. It did not occur to Arianna to try to resist him. She pressed her body against his, needing to be closer to him. Her hands were flat on his chest and she felt the heat of him through his shirt. Between kisses she snatched a breath and the spicy scent of his aftershave that assailed her senses sent another lick of fire through her.

His kiss transported her to another universe where only they existed—where there was only the hard wall of his muscular chest against her breasts and the sweet intoxication of his mouth on hers. She was lost instantly and utterly to his mastery, and she kissed him back mindlessly as the fire inside her became an inferno.

'We need to get out of here, *cara mia*.' Santino lifted his mouth from hers and whispered the words in her ear before he nipped her earlobe with his teeth.

She shivered with pleasure, but the spell he had cast on her broke, and reality hit like a sharp slap. It was bad enough knowing that his husky endearment was a lie and she was not his darling. But, worse still, they had been all over each other like a pair of teenagers while they'd been on the dance floor, in full view of four hundred or so party guests. Once again she was the centre of attention and it was a small mercy that the paparazzi were not around to snap pictures of her shameful behaviour. It was that thought that made her stiffen and pull out of Santino's arms.

'Aren't you worried that some of the other guests might post pictures of us on social media?' She was pleased that she managed to inject a note of mocking amusement into her voice to disguise the shame and hurt that coiled through her like a poisonous serpent. 'And if the tabloids got hold of the photos I'm sure my father wouldn't be too impressed, as he is paying you to keep me out of the limelight.'

Santino frowned. 'Arianna...'

'Leave me alone.' Tears stung her eyes and she blinked hard. She would rather die than let him see that if he cut her she would bleed the same as any other mortal. She heard him swear, but she'd already spun away from him and was weaving a path through the crowded dance floor, heading for the exit.

Outside the front of the club the paparazzi had dispersed. Behind her she heard Santino say urgently, 'Arianna, wait...' But she ignored him and hurried away from the brightly lit street.

Humiliated and desperate to be alone, she headed past the harbour, which at the height of the summer was full of yachts and motor cruisers. As she walked farther away from the town, the clinking sound of the yachts' rigging was a strangely mournful sound. A figure detached from the shadow of a doorway and walked past Arianna. She caught sight of the man's face in the light from the street lamp and had an odd feeling that she had seen him before somewhere.

When she reached the little beach area at the far end of the harbour, she took off her high-heeled sandals and walked along the shoreline, where the waves rippled over her feet. Her lips were still stinging from Santino's kiss and her insides squirmed as she recalled her wanton response to him. She hated him, she thought angrily, and she didn't understand why he affected her so much.

'*Signorina, per favore*, you have a light for my cigarette?'

The voice that came out of the darkness was strangely familiar. She whirled round to see the man who had passed her on the street a few moments ago. Now she recognised him as the jet-skier who had caused the accident the previous day. With him was a second man, and as the moon slid out from behind a cloud she realised that he was the steward from Jonny's yacht who had made her feel uncomfortable.

'No, I don't smoke,' she said loudly, hoping that there might be other people nearby who would hear her. The two men did not move away and Arianna's heart beat a frantic rhythm in her chest with the realisation that she was alone on the dark, deserted beach. She stumbled as the waves swirled around the hem of her ball gown. The men were both stockily built and rough-looking, and when they moved menacingly towards her she took another step backwards into the sea. 'What do you want?' she demanded fearfully.

CHAPTER SIX

SANTINO'S FEET POUNDED on the road, echoing the pounding of his heart as he raced towards the harbour. He hadn't seen which way Arianna had gone when she'd left the club, but he had been alerted by her scream, and as he ran he cursed himself for allowing her out of his sight. Again.

'Arianna, where the hell are you?'

In the moonlight he saw her tearing across the beach and relief hit him like a punch in his gut. He jumped down onto the sand and ran towards her, catching her when she threw herself into his arms. Her breath came in harsh gasps and her slender body shook as she burrowed into his shirt front.

'*Cara*, what happened?' He slid his hand beneath her chin and tilted her face up. The shimmer of tears in her eyes tugged on emotions he'd buried inside him when he had stood at his mother's graveside and vowed never to allow himself to care so deeply ever again.

She struggled to draw a breath. 'Two men approached me, and one of them grabbed my arm, but I managed to get away. I hid behind some boats on the beach, and the men must have heard you shouting my name, and they ran off. He tore my dress.' Arianna's voice wobbled and Santino saw that the shoulder strap on her dress was hanging by a thread. Violent anger surged through him but he ruthlessly controlled it and stroked his hand over her hair as if he were soothing a frightened colt.

'I'm sure the man who grabbed me was the jet-skier who ran into me and Hugo,' she said shakily. 'The other man works as a steward on Jonny's yacht. I noticed yesterday that he kept staring at me.'

Santino peered across the dark beach. A storm was brewing and the moon had disappeared behind clouds. Luckily Arianna had managed to hide from the men. But the scar on the back of his neck prickled and his instincts warned him that her safety was still threatened. He held her tighter when he felt a shudder run through her.

'Thank goodness you arrived when you did.' She managed a faint smile and Santino was struck by her courage. He would have expected her to be hysterical, but although clearly shaken she remained calm. 'It's the second time in two days that you've rescued me. Maybe I do need a bodyguard to keep me out of trouble after all,' she said ruefully.

His jaw clenched. He had promised Arianna's father that he would not tell her about the plot to kidnap her, but he had compromised her safety. He could not risk taking her back to Villa Cadenza—and he was grimly aware that his lack of control when he had kissed her had sent her running out of the nightclub and into danger.

Pulling his phone from his jacket, Santino made a brief call to Paolo, an old friend from his childhood. Earlier in the day he had arranged for Paolo to bring his boat across to the Amalfi coast from Sicily in case the kidnap threat escalated and he needed to get Arianna away quickly. That scenario had just become a reality, and once again he was furious that he had allowed himself to be distracted from his duty of protecting her.

'Come on, we should go,' he told her, trying to hide his concern that the two men—maybe there were more of them—could be close by.

'I left my shoes on the sand.' She resisted his attempt to lead her away from the beach. 'They're designer and cost a fortune. Why can't I go and find them? The men have gone, and I don't suppose they meant any harm. I allowed my imagination to run away with me,' Arianna argued when he clamped his arm around her waist and half-carried her along the jetty, past the boats moored on either side.

Behind him Santino heard the screech of tyres on the road, and when he looked back over his shoulder he saw four men jump out of a car and sweep a powerful flashlight over the boats in the harbour. He swore. 'Forget the damned shoes. We need to go now.'

'Go where?' Arianna's eyes were huge in her pale face when he halted next to a motor cruiser. 'Santino, what is going on? I'm not getting on a boat. I want to go back to Villa Cadenza.'

'It's too dangerous for you to return to the villa.' He heard footsteps walking fast along the jetty and realised he had no choice but to act. '*Cara*, you have to trust me,' he said before he scooped her off her feet and leapt aboard the cruiser with her in his arms. Paolo had already untied the ropes that secured the boat to the jetty and was waiting in the cockpit with the engine running. Santino called to him, and moments later the boat headed towards the harbour exit.

'Put me down!' Arianna thumped her fists on his chest when he carried her down the steps into the salon. He swore as he deposited her on the sofa.

'Take it easy, you little wildcat.'

The gold flecks in her eyes gleamed with temper. 'What do you mean "take it easy"? This evening I have been physically assaulted by two strangers and kidnapped by my bodyguard.'

Santino dragged his gaze from the jerky rise and fall of her breasts framed so perfectly by her gold dress. 'I'm not kidnapping you,' he said gruffly. 'I'm taking you to my home in Sicily where I will be better able to protect you from the mafia gang who are determined to kidnap you and demand a multi-million-pound ransom from your father for your release.'

She stared at him, the disbelief on her face turning to something warier when he held her gaze. 'That story sounds very far-fetched.'

'Why? Your father is immensely wealthy and your regular appearances in the tabloids made it easy for the gang to track your where-abouts. They have watched you for more than a year and know that you spend every sum-mer in Positano. They know who your friends are, and one of the gang applied for a job as a steward on your friend Jonny's yacht. When you went out on the jet-ski yesterday, the stew-ard alerted the other gang members, who were on a boat near to where the *Sun Princess* had dropped anchor.'

'How do you know all this?' Arianna bit her lip, drawing Santino's attention to her mouth, and he remembered how soft it had felt beneath his when he'd kissed her. Adrenalin was still pumping through his body, heightening his senses and inflaming his desire for her.

Cursing silently, he stripped off his jacket and loosened his bow tie before he crossed the salon to the bar. 'I don't know about you but I could do with a drink.' Alcohol might anaesthetise him to her sensual allure.

She shook her head when he held up a bottle of whisky. 'Could I have some water, please?'

He took a bottle of water from the fridge, poured himself a large whisky and walked back to sit down next to her on the sofa that ran along one wall of the salon. The single malt was smoky and mellow, and he took a long sip.

'I found out about the plot to kidnap you while I was working undercover to infiltrate a gang of drug smugglers in southern Italy. The authorities were unable to contact you to warn you of the threat, so they alerted your father, and Randolph subsequently hired me as your bodyguard. The Italian police are doing their best to hunt down the gang members and arrest them, but until that happens you are in danger.' He raked his fingers through his hair. 'The best way I can protect you is to hide you in Sicily where the kidnappers won't think of looking for you.'

'Why didn't you tell me?' She looked stunned, but almost immediately her chin came up and she glared at him. 'You had no right to keep that information a secret from me.'

'Your father thought it best that you did not know. He was concerned about how you would cope with the kidnap threat because he thinks you are emotionally fragile following the drug overdose you took a year ago.'

'I did *not* take an overdose,' she said sharply. 'At least, not the way my father implied.' The gold flecks in her eyes flashed again. 'I accidentally took too much of a strong flu remedy and was admitted to hospital after the housekeeper found me unconscious. I ended up in intensive care when I developed pneumonia. I was in hospital for five weeks, including for my birthday, but Randolph didn't visit or phone me once. I doubt he was even aware of how ill I was.'

The tremor in her voice tugged on something deep inside Santino that he was determined to ignore. He tore his gaze away from Arianna's mouth and drained his glass before he stood up and went to pour himself another drink.

'My father's indifference was proof, if I'd needed it, that he doesn't care about me,' she said dully.

'If that was true, why did he hire me to be your bodyguard?'

'If I was kidnapped it would create negative publicity likely to affect the value of Fitzgerald Design's shares when the company is floated on the stock market. Also, my father would loathe having to pay a ransom. Money is the only thing he cares about.' Her mouth trembled and she quickly pressed her lips together. 'I'm not even certain that he *would* pay the kidnappers to secure my release.'

'Of course he would,' Santino said roughly. 'Your father is not an ogre.'

'I recently discovered that he had bribed my mother not to seek custody of me after my parents divorced. Not because he wanted me, but because he is obsessively controlling.' She gave a bitter laugh. 'Randolph can be charming when he wants something. It would certainly suit him to hire an ex-SAS serviceman to foil a plot to kidnap the daughter he regards as a nuisance.' Her expression became speculative. 'I would be interested to know just how my father persuaded you to take the job of my bodyguard.'

She jumped to her feet and her temper exploded. Even the gossamer layers of her gold dress seemed to shimmer with fury. 'You should have told me the truth instead of treating me like a child.'

'You behaved like a child,' he countered harshly, trying to ignore the stab of guilt in his gut that she was right. 'You were determined to defy me.'

'Because I believed you had been sent by my father to control me. And maybe *that* is the truth here. I only have your word that a mafia gang are plotting to kidnap me.'

'What do you think the men on the beach wanted, Arianna?'

She paled, and guilt corkscrewed through him again. She had been through enough tonight, and he didn't know why he felt an overwhelming need to take her in his arms and comfort her. 'I can show you the email I received earlier this evening from the Italian police,' he said. 'I thought I recognised one of the stewards on Jonny's yacht. The police ran a check on him and confirmed that he is one of the gang members.'

'I see.' She sank down onto the sofa as if her legs would not hold her up. Her teeth gnawed her lower lip, making him want to lean forward and soothe the place with his tongue. She had driven him crazy all evening when he'd watched her dance with an endless stream of young men at the party. Popinjays all of them, insulated from the harsh realities of life by wealth and privilege, as Arianna herself was. It was odd, then, his idea that she did not fit in with her crowd of friends. That sense of alienation was something Santino remembered when his family had moved from Sicily to a small Devon village.

He swirled the amber liquid in his glass and asked himself why he was looking for hidden depths to Arianna that might indicate there was more to her than the spoilt party princess and tabloid darling. Why did he even care? He frowned. The insights she'd given about her relationship with her father had been surprising. Could it be that her attention seeking was a deliberate ploy to disguise the vulnerability that he'd glimpsed occasionally?

Annoyed by his train of thought, and more by his damnable fascination with her beautiful body, he stood up. Arianna was searching for something in her evening purse and pulled out a packet of pills.

'They're painkillers,' she explained when his eyes narrowed. 'I suffer from migraines, often brought on by stress,' she said pointedly. 'Do you have any idea how long I'll have to stay in Sicily?'

He shrugged. 'It could be a few weeks before the Italian police are able to arrest all the gang members.'

'Weeks! I assumed it would be a matter of days. It's crucial that I return to London by the middle of September for Fashion Week.'

'Your attendance at a fashion show is, of course, crucial,' he said sardonically. 'I'll tell the police they need to work faster so that your hectic social life isn't disrupted.'

As Santino strode up the steps and onto the

deck, he wondered why he had thought that there might be more to Arianna than vanity. She was a beautiful, empty shell, and he couldn't understand why he was disappointed or what he had hoped for.

He stepped into the motor cruiser's cockpit and chatted with Paolo. It was good to catch up on news about old friends, and he admitted to himself that he was glad of an excuse to return to Sicily. His family home, Casa Uliveto, was the only thing that he permitted himself to love, apart from his sister.

Santino regarded the first fifteen years of his life as a golden time before everything had changed. His mother had died and his father had sunk into a deep depression. It had scared him when he was a teenager to see how love and grief had destroyed Antonio. In truth the idea that love could have such a powerful effect still scared him far more than when facing his own mortality on the battlefields in Afghanistan.

Restlessly he headed back down to the salon, assuring himself that this need he had to be near Arianna was simply because she was his responsibility. His mouth twisted as he thought how much she would hate that. Her fierce independence surprised him as much as her fiery temper excited him. She was beautiful when she was angry and exquisite when she was asleep. Santino came to an abrupt halt in the doorway of the salon and stared at her slender form stretched out on the sofa.

She was lying on her side and the upper slopes of her breasts were pushed above the neckline of her dress, reminding him of perfect, round peaches that he longed to taste with his tongue. The side split in her long skirt had fallen open to reveal one slender, silky-smooth thigh. Her sensuality called to him like a siren's song, but the way she slept with her hand tucked beneath her cheek and her lips slightly parted was curiously innocent.

Even while Arianna was asleep she sent out conflicting messages, Santino thought grimly. Was she the shameless It Girl who played to the paparazzi? Or was that the lie, and was the ethereal creature who aroused his protective instincts—and aroused a lot more besides, he acknowledged self-derisively—the real Arianna Fitzgerald?

He looked over at the bar. The single malt offered a tempting escape from the mess inside his head but he resisted. Memories of seeing his father slumped in a chair, surrounded by empty cider cans and too drunk at three o'clock in the afternoon to be able to collect Gina from school, had taught Santino that alcohol did not provide salvation. He picked up his jacket and draped it over Arianna to keep her warm—not to save himself from the temptation of her delectable body.

And that, he thought grimly, was the biggest lie of all.

Sunlight slanting through the shutters cast stripes across the bedspread. Arianna opened her eyes and looked around the unfamiliar room, and her memory slowly returned. She was at Santino's villa in Sicily and this was his sister's bedroom. He had told her that Casa Uliveto had been his childhood home and his father had kept the house when the family had moved to England. Santino had explained that

Gina lived in New York and was not planning to visit in the next few months.

She sat up cautiously. Her head still felt delicate after the migraine attack that had started on the boat that had brought her and Santino to Sicily. The strong painkillers she'd taken had knocked her out and she remembered little of the journey. She vaguely recalled that Santino had carried her off the boat and across a beach to some steps that led up to the house. But she had been half-asleep and hadn't taken much notice of her surroundings, although she had been aware of his strong arms around her as he'd carried her, and the steady thud of his heart beneath her ear when she'd rested her head on his chest.

He had brought her to the bedroom, and she'd been sufficiently awake to take off her dress before she'd climbed into bed and immediately fallen back to sleep. She squinted at her watch and was shocked to find that it was nearly eleven a.m. No wonder her stomach felt hollow. Her feet met the cool floor tiles when she slid out of bed. The room's décor of whitewashed walls, dark wood furniture and soft blue bedding was simple but pretty, and the muted colour scheme was repeated in the en suite bathroom.

Arianna caught sight of herself in the mirror above the sink and grimaced to see her tangled hair and smudges of mascara on her cheeks. She never went to bed without first removing her make-up and using a variety of expensive potions on her skin. But the only items she'd brought with her in her little gold evening bag were a toothbrush, a mini perfume spritzer and a lip gloss. She didn't even have any shoes, she thought, remembering her beautiful designer sandals that she'd left behind on the beach in Amalfi.

It felt strangely liberating to have no possessions. At Lyle House and at Villa Cadenza her wardrobes were bursting with clothes, many of which she'd never worn. Shopping had filled the empty hours of every day, but the truth was that all the clothes, shoes and luxury toiletries that she'd paid for with a swipe of her credit card hadn't eased the emptiness inside her.

A shudder ran through her when she thought of the two men who had approached her on the beach after she'd run out of the nightclub. It had been a frightening experience but she'd assumed that the men were drunk and hadn't meant any real harm. Learning that they belonged to a mafia gang and had intended to kidnap her made the incident much more terrifying. If Santino had not found her in time, she could have been kidnapped and her life would have been in danger. The recent news story about a well-known footballer's wife, who had been snatched and then murdered by her kidnappers after her husband had involved the police, was a grim reminder that the mafia was utterly ruthless.

Her shoulder was stinging, and when she looked in the mirror she saw a jagged red weal on her skin. She remembered that the man who'd grabbed hold of her had been wearing a ring and she'd felt it cut into her. Nausea swept through her. She felt dirty and tainted, and with another shudder she hurried into the shower and scrubbed every inch of her body with a bar of lemon-scented soap.

Santino had told her that his sister kept a few items of clothes at the house and wouldn't mind if Arianna borrowed them. It was that or wear her ball gown, she acknowledged as she put on a pair of bleached denim shorts and a sleeveless cinnamon-coloured top made of a silky material that clung rather too lovingly to her breasts. It was lucky that she and Gina Vasari were the same dress size, she thought.

A pair of leather flip-flops that she found in the wardrobe fitted her. The lack of a hairdryer or straighteners meant that her hair dried naturally into loose curls. Studying her reflection in the mirror, she felt oddly vulnerable with her face bare of make-up. She felt naked without her favourite scarlet lipstick, and annoyingly she found herself wondering what Santino would think of her now that she looked ordinary instead of glamorous.

Arianna's heart skipped a beat when she went downstairs and found him in the kitchen. Like her, he was wearing denim shorts, and his black T-shirt was moulded to his impressive six-pack. She had followed the smell of bacon frying and her stomach growled as she watched him load two plates with bacon, eggs and mushrooms.

He gave her a searing look as she hovered uncertainly in the doorway. 'The only thing I liked when I moved to Devon as a teenager was an English cooked breakfast,' he told her as he pushed a plate across the table towards her. 'Help yourself to coffee.'

'I'm starving,' she confessed, pulling out a chair.

'Me too,' he drawled. The blatant suggestion in his voice brought her skin out in goose bumps, and the gleam in his eyes made her blush as he raked his gaze over her and she felt her nipples tighten. She hadn't worn a bra beneath her ball gown yesterday evening, and there hadn't been one among Gina's clothes for her to borrow. The silky material of the shirt brushing against her bare breasts with their taut, sensitive peaks felt deliciously sensual and made her intensely aware of her femininity.

Santino took his place opposite her at the table and picked up his knife and fork, but his eyes did not leave her face. 'You look very lovely this morning, Arianna,' he said gruffly.

Was he joking? Self-consciously she ran her

fingers through her riot of curls. 'I'm not wearing make-up.'

'You don't need it. Your skin is beautiful.' He broke off abruptly and she had the impression that he was annoyed with himself. Flustered and agonisingly aware of him, she dropped her gaze from his harshly handsome face and tried to concentrate on eating her breakfast.

'This is good,' she murmured after a couple of mouthfuls of crisp bacon. 'Where did you learn to cook?'

'The army taught me to be self-sufficient, but I'm not an expert chef by any stretch of imagination. My sister is a much better cook than me.'

She speared a mushroom. 'Why did you leave the army?'

'I'd served in the Parachute Regiment for ten years, including three tours of duty in Afghanistan, and I felt it was time to do something different.' He picked up his cup and took a gulp of coffee. 'A good friend of mine had been badly injured and Mac was invalided out of the army at the same time as I left. We decided to go into business together.'

'Doing what?' she asked curiously.

'My father had opened a delicatessen in Devon, specialising in selling olive oil that comes from the olive groves here at Casa Uliveto. Dad took little interest in the shop or anything else after my mother died. It was close to bankruptcy when I took it over but I managed to turn the business around. Mac and I ran it together until he left to pursue other interests.'

Arianna found it hard to picture Santino running a shop. It seemed rather ordinary for such an extraordinary man. 'I know from my father that you were in the SAS,' she murmured.

He shrugged, and she sensed he was reluctant to talk about his time in the special forces but she couldn't stem her curiosity. Her eyes were drawn to the tattoo of a snarling tiger on his arm. 'Does your tattoo have special significance?'

He nodded. 'I took part in a special mission in Helmand, codenamed Tiger. Those of us who survived had the tattoo done in honour of the men who lost their lives or suffered life-changing injuries.' His voice was flat and devoid of emotion but Arianna noticed a nerve jump in his cheek.

'The scar on your back.' she murmured. 'Did you receive it in Afghanistan?' She had been shocked when she'd seen the jagged scar that ran from his shoulder blade up to his neck and disappeared beneath his hairline.

Santino had stiffened when she'd mentioned his scar, and she thought he wasn't going to answer, but then he said, 'My patrol was ambushed by sniper fire,' he said at last in a taut voice. 'I was hit. It was bad luck that the bullet struck me at a point where I wasn't protected by my body vest. I would certainly have died if Mac hadn't dragged me out of the line of fire. But the area was strewn with landmines and one step in the wrong place could be fatal. In Mac's case, both his legs were blown off when an explosive device detonated.'

'It must have been terrible.' Arianna did not know what to say that wouldn't sound inane.

'Helmand was hell,' Santino told her savagely. 'You can have no idea of the guilt I feel knowing that my best friend can never walk again.'

Startled by the rawness in his voice, she murmured, 'You can't blame yourself. It was Mac's decision to go to your aid.'

His jaw clenched and Arianna sensed that he controlled his emotions with an iron will. 'Of course I blame myself,' he told her grimly. 'Mac didn't even know that I was alive when he ran across to me. If he had left me where I'd fallen he wouldn't be confined to a wheelchair for the rest of his life.'

Impulsively, Arianna reached across the table and covered Santino's hand with her own. Her eyes softened with compassion. 'What would you have done if the roles had been reversed? I don't believe that you would have left your friend to die.'

He frowned. 'Of course not.'

'If you had lost your limbs while saving Mac's life, would you blame him for your injuries?'

'No, I would be glad that he was alive.' He exhaled heavily. 'I see where you are going with this.' He moved suddenly and caught her fingers in his. 'I had not expected such insight from someone who spends her life shopping and socialising.' He looked down at her small hand in his much larger one and rubbed his thumb over the pulse that was beating frantically in her wrist. 'I am intrigued to know, who is the real Arianna Fitzgerald?'

'Just because I go to a lot of parties doesn't mean that I can't feel sympathy.' Desperate to hide the hurt she felt at his comment, Arianna said flippantly, 'Perhaps if the tabloids knew there was another side to me they would label me "the tart with a heart of gold".'

She snatched her hand out of his and continued to eat her breakfast, but her appetite had faded. Santino refilled both their coffee cups and leaned back in his chair, studying her intently, as if he was trying to fathom her out.

'Why was a Devon shopkeeper trying to infiltrate a gang of drug smugglers in Italy?' Arianna asked him. Something about his story did not add up.

He laughed. 'As a matter of fact I sold the delicatessen business a while ago. Prior to that Mac had left the business to set up a private investigation agency. He's fifteen years older than me, and before joining the army he had been in the police force.' Santino's expression turned serious. 'Mac's younger sister died suspiciously and Mac was convinced that Laura's drug-dealer boyfriend was involved in her death. He discovered that the guy had links to the mafia in southern Italy and he asked me to infiltrate the gang with the aim of breaking up their drug-smuggling operation.'

'Wasn't that an incredibly dangerous thing to do? If your cover had been blown the gang might have killed you.'

He shrugged. 'There was an element of risk. But Mac was devastated by his sister's death, and I owed him. When I learned that the gang intended to kidnap a wealthy English heiress, your safety took precedence over Mac's desire for revenge on his sister's killers. But if the Italian police are successful in arresting the gang members there will hopefully be justice for Laura.'

Arianna swirled the coffee grounds around in the bottom of her cup while she mulled over everything he had told her. From the sound of it Santino's only intention had been—and still was—to protect her from the mafia gang who wanted to kidnap her. He hadn't been trying to control her behaviour and keep her out of the media spotlight as she had accused him of doing. Her problem was that she believed every man was a control freak like her father, she thought ruefully.

Santino was brave and honourable. He had risked his life to help his friend Mac, and he had been there to protect her every time she had needed him. It made her stroppy attitude towards him when they had been in Positano seem even more childish.

At least now the subterfuge was over. She couldn't even blame him for withholding the truth about the kidnap threat when he had been given misleading information from her father that she had supposedly taken a drug overdose. The weeks she had spent in hospital with pneumonia had been a horrible, frightening time and the fact that Randolph hadn't contacted her at all had forced her to accept that he would never be interested in her.

She looked over at Santino and her breath caught in her throat when his gaze trapped hers. He was impossibly handsome and his chiselled features—those slashing cheekbones and square jaw—were cruelly beautiful. The only slight softening was his sensual mouth, tilted upwards at one corner in a wry smile that made her wish he would walk around the table, pull her into his arms and kiss her with all the heat and hunger she could see in his glittering green eyes.

He had said he was intrigued to know who she really was. And here at his house in Sicily, away from her old crowd and the photographer's lenses, she did not have to pretend any more. Maybe she could prove to him that she was not the party princess and darling of the tabloids. What if she told him that she didn't want to be that person any more, and that actually she had never been the wild child with a scandalous reputation? Would he even care? And why did his approval matter so much to her?

The answer caused her heart to give a jolt. She was falling in love with Santino. She had known the moment she had met him that he could be dangerous to her peace of mind and she'd sensed that he had the power to hurt her.

But he also made her feel more alive than she had ever felt, and that feeling was as dangerously addictive as she suspected the enigmatic man who had stolen her heart could be.

CHAPTER SEVEN

'I NOTICED SOME art folders in my bedroom,' Arianna said, pulling herself together and replacing her coffee cup on the saucer. 'Do they belong to your sister?'

Santino nodded. 'Gina took a combined art and business degree before she moved to America to become a fashion buyer.'

She felt envious of Santino's sister. She wished she had studied art, but at eighteen she'd lacked the confidence to apply to universities after her governess had told her that she did not have the commitment to work for a degree. Typically, she had decided to fulfil Miss Melton's low opinion of her and had spent the next six years partying in those playgrounds of the super-rich—Monaco, St Bart's, Verbier and Aspen.

Her lack of business qualifications was

something else she needed to consider before she launched her own fashion label, Arianna acknowledged. She had never had to live within a budget before but she would need to make big financial decisions. A familiar sense of worthlessness descended over her. Setting up her own company seemed daunting and maybe she would fail. *But isn't failure better than never trying?* whispered a stubborn voice inside her. It was the conclusion she had come to a year ago when she had been in hospital fighting for her life. She had been given a second chance and was determined to make her life worthwhile.

'There's an empty sketchpad with your sister's art portfolio. Would it be okay if I used it?' She kept her voice casual. 'I might do a bit of drawing to pass the time.'

'I don't suppose Gina would mind if you use some of her old art stuff. But don't think that you can swan around while you are staying here,' Santino told her bluntly. 'Unlike the luxurious way of life you are used to, I don't employ an army of staff to cater to your whims, and I'm not going to run around after you. I'll expect you to pull your weight. I don't suppose you've spent a lot of time in a kitchen or learned how to cook, but you can wash the dishes. No, there's isn't a dishwasher,' he said drily when she glanced around the room. 'Welcome to the real world, *cara.*'

'I'm not completely useless,' she snapped, stung by his mocking tone. She certainly wasn't going to admit to him that she had never washed the dishes in her life. When she ate alone in the vast dining room at Lyle House, the butler whisked the plates away immediately after she had finished eating.

Santino seemed to have used every pan in the kitchen, no doubt on purpose, she thought darkly as she filled the sink with hot water and started on the mountain of washing up he had created. But after she'd washed the copper pans and dried them with a tea towel until they gleamed, before she hung them on hooks above the stove, she realised that she was enjoying pottering about. There was a sense of achievement in turning the disorder back into a clean and tidy kitchen. It gave her confidence that she would manage just fine when she moved into her own home in London, probably a rented flat, as she wouldn't be able to afford to buy somewhere while she was trying to establish her business.

Through the window she saw Santino chopping the wood that was used to fuel the kitchen stove. He had stripped off his T-shirt and his broad shoulders glistened with sweat. Arianna felt a melting sensation low in her belly, an ache that throbbed insistently as she imagined him holding her against his muscular body, touching her, kissing her...

She blushed furiously when he glanced towards the window and caught her watching him. But she didn't look away and neither did he. The unguarded expression in his eyes made the ache inside her pulse harder, hotter. Even when they were not in the same room sexual tension simmered between them and she had no idea how they were going to live together, possibly for weeks, without that tension exploding into raw passion.

She released her breath on a shaky sigh when Santino finally resumed chopping logs. She could stand there all day watching his rippling muscles beneath the sheen of his olive-gold skin but it seemed wiser to keep out of his way—although not because she was afraid of him. He had proved that he was committed to protecting her. It was her reaction to his smouldering sensuality that scared her.

He evoked a longing in her that she'd never felt for any other man, she admitted to herself as she walked back up the stairs to her bedroom. She needed something to distract her, so she settled down with the sketch pad and pencils she'd found. It was some time later when she heard a knock on the door, and her heart clattered against her ribs as she scrambled off the bed and crossed the room to open it.

Santino braced his arms on the door frame and scowled at her. 'Do you intend to hide up here and sulk for the rest of the day?'

For some reason his bad mood made her feel better, knowing that he was as disturbed by her as she was by him. 'I didn't realise I'd been working for so long.' A glance at her watch revealed that she had been absorbed in sketching designs for a good part of the afternoon.

His brows rose and he said sardonically,

'Working? I didn't realise you knew the meaning of the word.' He looked over her shoulder at the pages of sketches scattered on the bed and his scowl deepened. 'You mean you've been drawing pretty pictures of dresses.'

'They're sketches of designs that I plan to create back at my fashion studio in London,' she told him, irked by his mocking tone. She stood aside to allow him to enter the bedroom and he walked over and picked up a few of the sketches.

'I know nothing about art or fashion but these look very detailed.' He gave her an intent look, as if he was trying to fathom her out. 'So, you have a studio?'

It sounded more glamorous that it actually was, but Arianna wasn't going to explain that she had recently signed the lease on a space in an old warehouse. She was paying the rent with money she'd inherited from her grandmother and she was excited that it was the first step towards independence from her father.

Santino's expression became speculative. 'Are you trying to emulate your father or merely playing at being a fashion designer until you grow bored of it?'

'Certainly not. Randolph won't be involved in any way in my fashion business. He doesn't know anything about my plans.' She bit her lip. 'No one does. You are the first person I've told.' She was already regretting that she'd given away her secret, but she had been angered by Santino's assumption that she could not do anything by herself and was reliant on her father.

'I'm hoping to launch my fashion brand "Anna" at London Fashion Week in February next year—if I can find a financial backer prepared to invest in my business.' She was unaware of the flicker of doubt that crossed her face. 'The reason I want to attend Fashion Week this September is so that I can see what is trending in the fashion world and hopefully make some contacts.'

She waved her hand at the sketches on the bed. 'These are ideas I'm working on for the mid-season shows, known in the industry as Pre-Fall, which are held around the end of November. The British Fashion Council are offering an opportunity for new designers to present their work. It will give me a chance to gauge the reaction of fashion journalists and buyers to my designs, but I'll have to work fast to be ready in time. And it won't help if I'm stuck in Sicily for weeks,' she said ruefully.

She leaned over the bed to gather up the loose pages of her sketches and the wide neck of her shirt slipped down, baring one shoulder. Santino swore softly.

'How did you get that cut? It looks sore.'

'It's nothing,' she muttered. 'One of the men on the beach was wearing a ring and the edge of it scraped my shoulder when he tried to grab me.' She felt sick remembering the incident, and perhaps she paled, because Santino put his hand on her uninjured shoulder and pushed her gently down onto the bed.

'Sit there while I find some antiseptic lotion,' he commanded.

Once his self-assurance had seemed threatening to her lack of confidence but now she accepted his strength instead of resenting it. He strode into the bathroom and returned almost instantly carrying a first-aid kit, from which he took out a tube of cream.

'Hold still.' He unscrewed the cap and squeezed a little of the medication onto her shoulder. His touch was surprisingly gentle when he spread the cream over the cut.

Arianna had a sudden memory of when she'd been a little girl and her mother had cared for her grazed knees after she'd fallen off her bike. She had adored Celine, but the close bond between them had lessened when her father had insisted on sending her to a boarding school when she'd been eight. The older pupils had teased the younger ones who cried if they were homesick, and even at that young age she'd learned to hide her feelings behind a wall of bravado.

She could not understand why Santino's unexpected kindness made her eyes fill with tears. She tried to blink them away but a trickle of moisture slipped down her cheek.

'Does the cut hurt?' His concern tugged on her heart. She couldn't remember the last time someone had actually cared about her. Arianna shook her head, not trusting herself to speak.

He sat beside her on the bed and trapped her chin in his fingers, tilting her face up so that she could not evade his gaze. Something indefinable flickered in his green eyes as he brushed a tear away with his thumb. 'Don't cry, *piccola*,' he said softly.

She stared at his mouth as he brought it closer to hers and felt that inexplicable pull that had always existed between them. From the start there had been a connection, a mutual awareness, that they had both tried to deny. But she didn't want to fight him any more, Arianna admitted to herself. She wanted to throw herself into his fire and burn in the blaze of his smouldering sensuality.

He moved his hand from her jaw to caress her cheek and she felt his other hand slide into her hair. Her heart was beating so fast that she felt breathless, and something hot and urgent unfurled in the pit of her stomach when she glimpsed the hunger in his gaze seconds before he claimed her mouth with his and the world spun off its axis.

She tasted of honey, sweet and utterly addictive, and Santino could not resist her. He told himself that he had kissed her simply to comfort her, conveniently pushing aside the knowledge that *caring* was an emotion he avoided. The vulnerability he glimpsed in her chocolate-drop brown eyes stirred something inside him that he refused to acknowledge, much less define. Perhaps that air of loneliness about her was another illusion created by the smoke and shadows that was Arianna.

Right now she was real enough. Her lips were soft and moist beneath his and her warm breath filled his mouth. He wanted more, wanted her closer, and he lifted her across his lap and nearly lost it when her bottom pressed against the painfully hard ridge of his arousal. Her perfume teased his senses. She smelled of exotic flowers on a hot summer's day, and the lemon groves in his beloved Sicily, but her fragrance was as frustratingly elusive as the woman who curled her arms around his neck and wantonly pressed her breasts up against his chest.

He could feel the hard tips of her nipples, tight and hot, burning through his T-shirt. It didn't matter what Arianna was or what she was not. Right now she was in his arms and kissing him with a hunger that matched his own, and there was not a chance in hell that he would deny himself what he had wanted from the moment he'd set eyes on her. Arianna beneath him, on top of him. His fantasies about her had kept him awake at night, and he was done with trying to figure out why she fascinated him more than any woman ever had.

Without lifting his mouth from hers, he pushed his hand between their bodies and slipped it beneath her silky top, skimming his fingers over her stomach and up to capture one breast. He tested its weight in his palm and felt her shudder when he dragged his thumb over her nipple. Her skin was as soft as a peach and he had to taste her. Easing away from her a fraction allowed him to lift her shirt up and over her head, baring her breasts to him.

He gave a low growl of appreciation. She was perfection. Her creamy skin was satin-smooth and her breasts were round and firm, each pert mound adorned with a dusky pink nipple that tilted provocatively, inviting him to run his tongue over the tip. He was shocked to find that his hands were unsteady when he sank them into her glorious hair and let her silky curls slip through his fingers. Desire pounded an insistent drumbeat in his blood, and he knew from her rapid breathing and the slumberous heat in her eyes that her need was as great as his.

He shoved away the strange idea he'd had on previous occasions that her air of innocence was real. Stories of her excesses had filled too many gossip columns. Not that Santino cared. He enjoyed sex with women who were sexually confident. The sight of the cut on her shoulder made him hesitate, and perhaps he would have heeded the reminder that it was his duty to protect her if she hadn't dragged the hem of his T-shirt up his torso and run her hands over his chest.

'Witch,' he said hoarsely when she scraped her nails across his flat nipples, making him even harder, even hungrier for her. Unable to control his impatience, he tugged his shirt off before he bent his head to her breast, closing his mouth around her nipple and sucking. Hard. The effect on her was instant, but the audible catch of her breath…surely she could not have sounded startled? Once again Santino pushed the odd thought away and concentrated on pleasuring her breasts, rolling one nipple between his fingers while simultaneously lashing the other turgid peak with his tongue.

She arched backwards, offering her breasts to him, and he had never seen anything more beautiful than Arianna with her cheeks flushed with passion and her long hair—shades of chestnut and cinnamon—tumbling in a riot of loose curls down her back. The heat between them burned hotter and the world disintegrated. He tumbled them both down onto the mattress and propped himself up on one elbow while he skimmed his other hand down to the waistband of her denim shorts.

'Look at me,' he commanded, a question in his eyes when her lashes swept up and she met his gaze. She answered him by pulling his face down to hers and parting her lips with an eagerness that caused his heart to give a jolt as he kissed her again and again. He would never have enough of her. She was a siren luring him to his doom, but he didn't care about anything other than his need to possess her gorgeous body and seek salvation between her silken thighs.

He fumbled with the button and zip on her shorts, impatience making his movements un-characteristically clumsy. Finally, he tugged the denim shorts down her legs and sat back on his knees to admire the graceful lines of her slender figure, almost naked but for the tiny black knickers that hid her femininity from him.

Her eyes were huge and dark with desire, and Santino's gut clenched at the soft sound she made—half-protest, half-plea—when he leaned over her, braced his hands on either side of her on the bed and pressed his mouth against the scrap of black lace. The scent of her arousal filled his senses as he pushed the panel of her panties aside and ran his tongue over her slick, wet opening. Her molten heat was the sweetest nectar and he felt a quiver run through her when he delved deeper into her feminine core, lapping her, tasting her.

Arianna's husky gasps of pleasure almost sent Santino over the edge, but somehow he still retained enough control to remember that they were not in his bedroom, where he kept contraceptives. But his sister and her fiancé had stayed in this room when they had visited earlier in the summer. His heart kicked in his chest when he pulled open the bedside drawer and found a packet of condoms. He was so hard he thought he might explode, and he bit back a groan when his denim shorts snagged on his erection as he yanked them off, followed by his boxers.

He knelt back on the bed and looked down at Arianna. She was more beautiful than anything he had ever seen with her silky hair spread over the pillows and her big brown eyes lit with gold flames. The elegant lines and sensual curves of her body were a work of art, and his gut clenched in anticipation of her long, lissom legs wrapped around his back. Her pert breasts were firm yet soft, the colour of pale cream, each topped with a cherry-red nipple, and he bent his head and feasted on them, smiling when she bucked and moaned.

Next time he would take things more slowly and indulge in leisurely foreplay, he promised himself. But right now he was desperate to be inside her and he swiftly donned a protective sheath. He pulled her panties down her legs and ran his fingers over the neat vee of soft brown curls he'd exposed before he pushed her thighs apart. Supporting his weight on his elbows, he positioned himself over her and lowered his head to claim her mouth in a hungry kiss.

'I should probably tell you…' she whispered against his lips.

Dio! Had she changed her mind? His heart was thundering in his chest but somehow he held himself back. 'The only thing you need to tell me, *cara*,' he growled, 'is if you want this. One word—yes, or no?'

'Yes,' she said without hesitation.

Relief surged through him, adding to the potent heat in his groin. He didn't wait—couldn't, if he was honest. His desire for her consumed him and he slid his hands beneath her bottom to lift her hips towards him.

At last he was where he wanted to be—on the edge of heaven.

He surged forward and thrust into her. And stilled.

His shock turned to incomprehension and disbelief when she went rigid beneath him. The sharp cry she'd given at the moment he'd penetrated her had been of pain.

How the hell could Arianna be a virgin?

Guilt seared through him even as he felt the tension slowly seep from her body as her internal muscles stretched to accommodate him. He felt as though his aching shaft was encased in a velvet glove. Her slick heat enticed him to slide deeper into her. But he held back, just, his throat working as he swallowed hard. The craziest thing of all was the swift, fierce rush of triumph that swept through him, a possessiveness that shook him to his core and which he rejected absolutely. Sex and emotions was not a mix he had ever sought.

He withdrew from her, even though it was the hardest thing he had ever done. He did not know if it was disappointment or relief that darkened her eyes, and when she bit her lip the beast inside him roared. Cursing beneath his breath, he propped himself up beside her and trapped her gaze with his. 'Why?' he demanded tautly.

Something flickered on her lovely face, that hint of vulnerability that he now knew was real, he thought, guilt clawing through him again. 'Why was I a virgin, I suppose you mean?' she said in a low voice.

He gritted his teeth. 'You suppose right, *cara*. How could it be so, when stories of your affairs have littered the gutter press for years and provided cheap titillation for anyone who is interested?'

Colour ran along her exquisite cheekbones but she said defiantly, 'No one believes the rubbish printed in the tabloids.'

The implication that anyone who did was a fool was not lost on Santino, and with a flash of insight he realised that he had wanted to believe the worst of her to keep her at arm's length. 'What about when you defied me and left Villa Cadenza to go and meet your lover in Positano?' He recalled the scalding jealousy he'd felt, imagining her in bed with some guy.

'I was having sewing lessons with a seamstress in her workroom next door to the beauty salon.' She shrugged when his brows lowered. 'You were convinced that I must be having an affair because you believed my reputation as a tart was true.'

Santino sighed heavily, unable to deny her accusation. 'Did you never consider denying the things that were written about you or demand a retraction from the newspapers?'

She glanced at him from beneath her long eyelashes. Her wariness that he had assumed was an act now tugged on emotions he did not want to acknowledge. 'You'll laugh if I tell you the truth.'

'Try me,' he said gruffly.

'The only times my father ever phoned me were when some scandal or another about my private life made the headlines. He hated my notoriety, not because he cared about me, but because he feared it could have an adverse effect on the only thing he does care about, which is Fitzgerald Design.' She bit her lip. 'When I was a child, Randolph only noticed me when I behaved badly, so I carried on. But a year ago I decided that I can't spend the rest of my life seeking my father's attention.' Her rueful smile did not reach her eyes. 'I suppose I finally grew up.'

Santino ignored the complicated feelings that Arianna evoked in him. 'I haven't seen much evidence of that,' he mocked. 'You should have told me it was your first time.'

'I tried to...'

He swore, and colour ran under her skin, but her eyes flashed gold with temper. 'Would you have believed me?' she came back at him, fiery and proud. She sat upright and pushed a hand through her hair, drawing his eyes to the silky brown curls that tumbled over her breasts. Desire corkscrewed through him but he couldn't succumb to his hunger for her that made him feel hollow and aware of the gaping emptiness inside him. An emptiness that Arianna of all people could not fill. Whatever she thought of her father, Randolph had hired him to protect his daughter, and he would do his duty, Santino vowed silently.

'Why me?' he demanded.

She did not pretend to misunderstand him and her reply set off alarm bells inside his head. 'I knew I would be safe with you,' she said softly.

Safe! The word mocked him. 'Arianna...'

She interrupted him. 'From the start you have taken care of me.'

'It is my job to protect you,' he growled.

She shook her head. 'It's more than that and you know it. There is a connection between us.' Before he could deny it, she said fiercely, 'I wanted you to be the first.'

'And because you are Arianna Fitzgerald you decided that it is your unassailable right to have what you want, with no thought of the consequences,' he said furiously. 'You should have been honest instead of dumping your virginity on me and expecting—what?—that I would fall in love with you?'

He swung himself off the bed and pulled on his shorts, hardening his heart against her stricken expression. When had his *heart* got involved? he wondered blackly, feeling a beat of fear. He had decided a long time ago when his mother had died and his father had become a broken man that he was better off alone.

'A few minutes ago you wanted to make love

to me.' Arianna's voice pulled him from the past. 'I didn't think you would realise it was my first time, but I hadn't expected it to hurt as much as it did,' she admitted wryly.

Truly, she was going to kill him. 'I don't do love,' he told her bluntly. 'I wanted to have sex with you, and why wouldn't I? You are beautiful, and I thought you were experienced.' He tried to ignore his conscience that reminded him that he'd sensed an innocence about her that had baffled him.

He bent down to retrieve his shirt from the floor and pulled it on. When he turned back to face her he was relieved that she had tugged the sheet around her, hiding the temptation of her gorgeous body from his eyes, although nothing could erase the memory of how she had felt beneath him, so soft and pliant. Cursing silently, he strode across to the door.

'I understand what has happened,' he told her curtly. 'It's not uncommon for a client to develop a crush on the bodyguard assigned to protect them. It is my responsibility to take care of you until the kidnap threat is over. But you have a romanticised view of our relationship. Hopefully the situation will be resolved soon. I received an update from the Italian police that they are closing in on the gang, and when you leave here and return to your old life you will forget about me.'

'Do you really believe that, Santino?' From the other side of the room the gold flecks in Arianna's eyes flashed fiery bright. She knelt up on the bed and lowered the sheet, baring her breasts. Tossing her hair back over her shoulders, she put her hands on her hips, and the sheet slipped down to reveal her slim thighs and the sexy triangle of tight curls that hid her femininity. 'I know you want me.'

Despite himself, and his determination to resist her, Santino could not take his eyes from her. 'Beautiful' did not come near to describing her lush curves and the brazen, seductive promise of her exquisite body. But, as with everything to do with Arianna, that promise was a lie. She was innocent—or she had been, until he had taken her virginity, he thought grimly. *Dio*, she was something else for him to feel guilty about.

His muscles ached with tension as he fought

188 THE VIRGIN'S SICILIAN PROTECTOR

an internal battle with himself. He could cross the room in four strides and pull her into his arms, finish what he had started. Temptation pulsed hard and hot in his blood but he fought it. *It was his duty to protect her.* From herself if necessary, and especially from him, because, whatever Arianna was looking for, Santino knew he could not give it to her.

'You're wrong,' he told her impassively. 'I want a woman who understands the concept of sex without strings. Not someone who is needy and immature and who is looking for some sort of father figure to give her the attention she craves.' She blanched and he reminded himself that he was being cruel to be kind. The quicker he disabused Arianna of the idea that he was a heroic figure, the better for both of them. He stepped into the corridor and spoke to her over his shoulder. 'I suggest you put your clothes on and we will forget that any of this ever happened.'

CHAPTER EIGHT

SHE WAS SUCH an idiot! Fiery colour scorched Arianna's cheeks, making her feel even hotter than she already was, squashed into the over-crowded carriage on the Tube. It was more than four months since Santino had rejected her and decimated her pride. It had taken a long time for her to scrape herself off the floor, and she still had regular flashbacks to how she had wanted to die of embarrassment when she'd dragged a sheet around her naked body after he had turned her down.

A few moments ago, the sight of a tall, dark-haired man standing on the station platform had made her heart lurch, until he had turned around, and her stomach had swooped with disappointment that it wasn't Santino. She searched for his ruggedly handsome face ev-erywhere, even though she knew it was pointless to look for him in London. Presumably he was at his villa in Sicily, or in Devon, where he had owned a delicatessen shop. He hadn't told her what he did for a living since he'd sold the shop but maybe he had taken over his grandparents' farm.

Her heart gave a pang as she remembered his sexy grin when he'd confessed that he hadn't enjoyed milking cows. She had smiled back at him, her heart soaring because he'd shared something of himself with her, something that perhaps he had never told any of those women with whom he enjoyed sex without strings. She had stored every snippet of information she had learned about him in her mind, like a magpie hiding golden treasure in its nest. And at night her imagination ran riot as she pictured Santino's naked body, a masterpiece of powerful muscles and satiny, olive-gold skin, his broad chest covered with whorls of dark hairs that arrowed over his flat stomach and grew thickly around the base of his manhood.

The train pulled into the underground station and Arianna was glad to escape from the carriage before the heat inside her made her combust. But she could not stop her mind flitting back to the awful, awkward days at Casa Uliveto when she had been desperate to avoid Santino. Forgetting what had happened between them was impossible.

In the past, when her friends had talked about sex, she had tried to imagine a scenario when she finally lost her virginity. Ever the romantic, she had dreamed of giving herself to a man she trusted, and she'd thought she had found that person. But Santino's cruel rejection had blown apart her fantasy that he felt something for her. That he *cared* about her. He had reminded her that it was his job to protect her, and insisted that what she felt for him was a crush, as if she'd been a silly teenager mooning over pictures of her favourite pop star.

Repressing a shudder of shame, Arianna joined the queue of rush-hour commuters shuffling towards the escalator at London Bridge station. She checked the time, and her stomach nosedived as she realised that she was in danger of being late for the most important meeting of her life.

Her thoughts flicked back to Sicily. Thankfully her ordeal of living with Santino, and cringing with embarrassment whenever she'd walked into a room and found him there, had only lasted for a week. Early one morning he had knocked on her bedroom door, and she'd despised herself for the way her heart had leapt with hope that he had come to claim her because he could not resist her.

Instead he had informed her in a clipped voice that the Italian police had swooped on the mafia gang and arrested them. The kidnap threat was over, and he had chartered a private jet to take her to Positano or London, whichever she decided. It had been painfully obvious that he couldn't wait for her to leave, and Arianna had told herself that she'd imagined she'd glimpsed a feral hunger mixed with regret in his eyes before he had turned and walked out of the room.

She snapped back to the present as she emerged from the station and was met by an icy blast of wind that carried a mixture of rain and sleet. December had heralded the start of winter, and her elegant champagne-coloured skirt and jacket and matching four-inch stiletto heels offered no protection against the elements. She regretted that she hadn't taken a taxi across London, but now that she was living on a tight budget she couldn't afford luxuries such as taxis.

Fortunately, The Shard was close to the station, and as she hurried towards the building's entrance she looked up at the iconic skyscraper clad with glass that reflected the sullen grey skies above. Tiger Investments' offices were on the seventeenth floor, and Arianna took a deep breath and tried to calm her nerves when she exited the lift into the company's minimalist and very stylish reception area.

'I have an appointment to see Rachael Martin,' she told the stylish blonde receptionist after she'd introduced herself.

The young woman smiled. 'I'll let Rachael know you have arrived.'

While she waited, Arianna mentally ran through her presentation. She had been contacted by Tiger Investments after she had applied for funding for her fashion business through an angel investor network. She knew that angel investors were essentially private individuals or companies who provided capital for new businesses in return for equity. This was her chance to secure money that she needed to cover the huge costs involved in showing her designs at London Fashion Week.

She wondered how Rachael Martin, who she assumed headed the investment company, had become a successful businesswoman. Not for the first time Arianna was beset by doubts that she could establish her own fashion label in a highly competitive market place. But a stubborn belief that her designs were fresh and innovative meant that she pinned a smile on her lips when she heard her name.

'Miss Fitzgerald? I'm Rachael. If you would like to come with me, I'll take you to your meeting.' The woman who greeted her possessed a self-confidence that Arianna envied. She could do this, she told herself as she followed the other woman along a plush carpeted corridor, lifting a hand nervously to check that her chignon was in place before she stepped into a large room with glass walls and floor-to-ceiling windows. It was like being in a goldfish bowl, and heading straight for her was a predatory shark.

'What are you doing here?' Her heart slammed into her ribs as she stared at Santino. He looked different from the bodyguard she had known in Italy but no less handsome. Instead of jeans he wore a charcoal-grey suit, pale-blue shirt and a navy silk tie. The superbly tailored jacket emphasised the width of his shoulders and he was so devastatingly attractive in his formal clothes that she sucked in a sharp breath. 'Don't tell me that you work for Tiger Investments? The coincidence would be too ghastly,' she murmured, striving to sound flippant to disguise her shock.

'I *own* Tiger Investments,' he corrected her coolly.

'But… I thought that Rachael Martin…' Arianna glanced over her shoulder and discovered that the other woman had left the room.

'Rachael is my PA,' Santino told her. 'I asked her to arrange your visit because I thought you would refuse to meet me.'

In her mind Arianna pictured the tattoo of a tiger on Santino's bicep. There had been a clue in the name Tiger Investments, but honestly she had never expected to see him again. Thinking of his tattoo evoked memories of his naked, aroused body, which did nothing to restore her composure.

'You were right. We have nothing to say to one another.' Disappointment thickened her voice with the realisation that Santino had brought her here on false pretences. 'Is this another example of your cruelty—to get my hopes up that you would offer funding for my fashion company?'

His eyes narrowed on her face. 'You gave yourself to me, *cara*. Don't try to make out that you were a martyr,' he said softly.

She flushed as erotic images swirled in her mind of his whipcord body poised above her and his erection pushing between her legs. Molten heat pooled low in her pelvis and she hastily dropped her gaze from his.

Santino walked over to the sleek black-and-chrome desk that took up the whole of one corner of the office, but instead of sitting behind it he leaned his hip against the top and indicated the chair in front of the desk. 'Please, sit down—unless you prefer to stand while you give your presentation.'

'Is there any point?' Arianna felt a flare of frustration that she'd had a wasted journey. 'I'm looking for at least five hundred thousand pounds to launch my business, and I doubt that the proceeds from the sale of your delicatessen in Devon would allow you to make that level of investment.'

'My company, which traded under the brand name of Toni's Deli, was valued at two hundred and seventy-five million pounds when I sold the business.'

She sank down onto the chair. '*You* owned the Toni's Deli chain of shops? The brand is huge in the UK and Europe.'

He nodded. 'I built the company up from one poorly performing outlet that my father had opened in Exeter to over two thousand stores in seventeen international locations. I'd dabbled in investing in start-up companies, and eventually sold the delicatessen business so that I could set up Tiger Investments. The question is not whether I have enough money to invest in your business,' he said sardonically. 'You will have to prove to me that you have a product and business strategy that I believe will be successful.'

He straightened up, but instead of moving to sit behind his desk he pulled up a chair next to Arianna. She felt a betraying heat spread across her cheeks. Being this close to him made her heart race, and the spicy scent of his aftershave evoked memories of when she had been in his arms and he had kissed her with fierce passion. Seeing Santino again had been shocking enough, and learning that he was a millionaire entrepreneur had completely thrown her.

She fired up her laptop and opened the PowerPoint file containing her pitch deck that Jonny had helped her to create for her fashion label, Anna. 'You want to give a brief overview of your business model. Ten to fifteen slides that will make a great first impression,' Jonny had told her. 'Don't read from your script or you'll sound like a robot. And make eye contact with the person you are hoping to impress.'

No doubt it was sound advice, but Arianna's

mind had gone blank. She bit her lip when she accidentally brought up the wrong file. 'Sorry, just bear with me,' she muttered. She couldn't bring herself to look at Santino let alone make eye contact with him. The first slide flashed up on the screen and she dropped her pages of notes on the floor. Flustered, she leaned down to pick them up at the same time as he did, and their hands brushed, sending a sizzle of heat through her.

She had assumed that nothing could be more humiliating than when she had offered her body to Santino only for him to tell her that she was needy and immature. But she had been wrong, Arianna thought miserably fifteen minutes later, when she had finished delivering her presentation and stumbled to answer the questions he fired at her. She was angry with herself for making such a hash of it, and his silence shredded her nerves even more. 'Well, what do you think?' she asked nervously.

'I think that was the worst presentation I've ever sat through.' His blunt reply made her heart sink and, when she forced herself to look at him, she saw impatience glittering in his green eyes. 'Your marketing skills are, at best, questionable, and you seem to know nothing about PR and creating a brand.'

He leaned back in his chair and hooked his ankle across his other thigh, looking the epitome of a hard-nosed, highly successful entrepreneur. 'Your *only* saving grace,' he said curtly, 'is that I believe you have a good product. My sister saw your Pre-Fall collection last month at a show arranged by the British Fashion Council to present emerging designers. I think I mentioned that Gina is a senior buyer for a New York department store. She knows the fashion industry, and she was genuinely excited by your designs.'

Arianna's spirits, which had sunk to the pointed toes of her designer heels, cautiously lifted. 'Does that mean you will consider investing in Anna?'

Santino stood up and strode over to the window. The usually spectacular view across the city was shrouded in thick cloud, and the rain beating against the glass made him long for the heat and sun of a Sicilian summer's day. But his beloved Casa Uliveto was no longer the restful bolthole where he could relax.

After he had sent Arianna away he'd assumed that he would forget about her fairly quickly. But she had constantly been in his thoughts, and at night he'd been kept awake by memories of how she had knelt on the bed— naked and so goddamned beautiful that he ached thinking about her—and offered herself to him. There had always been a danger, when he'd arranged to meet Arianna today, that he would think with a certain part of his anatomy that was as hard as a spike beneath his trousers, rather than with his head, he acknowledged.

Her business plan was laughable, and he should send her packing, but his instincts told him that her fashion label Anna had huge potential. He had noticed Arianna's name when he'd reviewed start-up companies on an angel investor network. When his sister had come to London last month he had asked Gina to attend the Pre-Fall shows and give an opinion on Arianna's designs.

'She is the most exciting new designer this year, perhaps this decade,' Gina had assured him. 'Arianna Fitzgerald has phenomenal talent, which I suppose is not surprising, when you consider that her father is one of the greatest fashion designers in the world.'

Santino swung round from the window and studied Arianna, irritated by his body's involuntary reaction to her as desire corkscrewed through him. She was even lovelier than he remembered. His eyes were drawn to her long legs encased in sheer tights. Her vertiginous heels added at least four inches to her height. The fitted jacket of her elegant suit emphasised her narrow waist that he remembered he could span with his two hands. She had unfastened the jacket's buttons, and her breasts were high and firm beneath her silk blouse.

So much for his belief that he had managed to get her out of his system, he thought grimly. One reason for meeting her had been to test his immunity to her sensual allure. The ache of his arousal was mocking proof that he had failed.

'I don't understand why your presentation did not include the fact that your father is Randolph Fitzgerald,' he said abruptly. 'Or for that matter why you are seeking investment in your business when your father could bankroll your fashion label.'

She stiffened at his mention of her father. 'I've had no contact with Randolph since I returned to London, and he is not involved in any way in my business plans.'

'Linking your fashion label to Fitzgerald Design would be an excellent way to promote Anna. It doesn't make sense not to utilise your association with your father.'

'No.' Arianna jumped to her feet. 'Anna is *my* label. The designs are entirely my work, and if I succeed it will be on my own merits, not because of who my father is.'

'And what if you fail?'

'I won't fail.' The gold flecks in her eyes flashed with determination. 'I know my designs are good. My Pre-Fall collection received excellent reviews and my Autumn/Winter collection for next year, that I am working on to showcase at London Fashion Week in February, is even better,' she said passionately.

Dio, he wanted to burn in her fiery passion.

The throb in Santino's groin intensified as he imagined Arianna's naked, creamy pale limbs spread across the black glass surface of his desk. It would be easier if he could dismiss her business ideas as unlikely to succeed. Then he could simply invite her to dinner and take her to bed, and he was confident that within a month he'd have grown bored of her, which invariably happened with the women he bedded.

But his gut told him to put his money into Anna, and his instincts had always proved right in the past, which was how he had become a self-made millionaire. He walked back across the room, picked up her presentation notes that she had left on the desk and dropped them into the wastepaper bin.

'That's what I think of your business plan,' he told her, trying to ignore the inexplicable tug he felt in his chest when he studied her crestfallen face. 'I am prepared to make an investment of half a million pounds in your fashion label, but I want a forty percent stake in the company.'

He watched her eyes widen. The flush of rose-pink that winged along her exquisite cheekbones made her prettier than ever, and Santino threw himself down into the chair behind his desk to conceal the bulge of his arousal beneath his trousers. 'Also,' he said gruffly, 'you will have to improve your marketing skills. I'll expect you to meet me twice a week so that we can work on business strategies and promotion ideas.'

'I won't have time,' she argued. 'I was planning to employ staff to deal with PR and the business side of the company, to allow me to focus on my role as creative director.' Her mouth turned down at the corners and Santino didn't know whether he wanted to shake some sense into her or kiss the sulky pout from her lips. The latter was a serious contender, he acknowledged heavily.

'You can't just do the fun stuff,' he told her impatiently. 'What I learned from running my delicatessen company is the necessity to know and understand every aspect of the business. Creating a product, whether it is clothes, cars or dog food, is the easy part. The hard work is persuading people to buy your product rather than a competitor's.' He stood up to indicate that the meeting was over. 'I'll have my legal team draw up a contract for you to sign, and money will be transferred into your business account.'

Arianna also rose to her feet. She was poised and elegant, making him long to ruffle her and unearth the passionate woman he had discovered in Italy. 'I realise that I need a better understanding of running a business, and I am willing to learn everything you can teach me,' she said softly.

Dio, had he imagined there was a double-edged meaning in her words? Erotic images filled his mind of the things he would like to teach her in his bed. She smiled and Santino's breath was squeezed from his lungs. It was not the perfunctory smile that had graced the tabloids when she had been endlessly photographed by the paparazzi. It was the smile he had seen once before when they had been on the beach in Positano. Open and unfeigned, it lit up her face and made the gold flecks in her brown eyes gleam with the warmth of the Sicilian sun.

It hit Santino with the force of a meteor

strike that it wasn't Sicily he had missed for the past four months but Arianna. She held out her hand and, as he curled his fingers around hers, a jolt of electricity shot up his arm and he cursed silently.

'So we have a deal,' she murmured. 'Thank you. I promise you won't regret it.'

Too late, he thought grimly. He was already regretting his decision to get involved with Arianna's business. But he could not make it personal, and he was determined to keep their relationship on a professional footing. He didn't want to feel the confused emotions that she evoked inside him. He did not want to *feel*, full stop.

He watched the sexy sway of her bottom beneath her tight-fitting skirt as she walked out of his office and ordered himself to get a grip. But the scent of her perfume lingered in the room for the rest of the day, heating his blood so that he could not concentrate on work. He reminded himself that he could retract his offer to invest in her fashion label. She would find another investor, and he would go back to being comfortably numb, which was how he preferred to live his life.

Santino's jaw clenched. The SAS had the motto 'Who Dares Wins'. Was he seriously considering pulling out of a good investment opportunity because he was afraid of getting involved with Arianna? He was confident he could handle his inconvenient attraction to her—and if not, if all else failed, he would have to get his hands on her and resolve his fascination by taking her to bed.

CHAPTER NINE

THREE FRUSTRATING WEEKS later Santino was forced to admit that he had made a serious error of judgment. However, the problem was not his investment in Arianna's fashion label.

The official launch of Anna would be the debut runway collection at London Fashion Week's spring show, early in the new year. There had been a buzz of interest from fashion journalists in the wake of Arianna's Pre-Fall showcase, and her client list was growing quickly. So much so that Santino had suggested she should move into a larger studio so that she could employ pattern cutters and seamstresses. At the moment she did everything from designing clothes through to making the final product, and he knew that she often worked until eight or nine o'clock at night.

In all honesty he had been impressed by

her work ethic and drive to succeed. At their twice-weekly meetings, where he was giving her a crash course in business operations and marketing strategy, she had shown that she was fiercely intelligent and quick to learn. Santino realised that he looked forward to those meetings. Arianna's dry wit often made him laugh. She was also a good listener and he'd found himself opening up to her in a way that he had never done to anyone else.

He'd told her things that he had buried deep in his subconscious about what he had witnessed in Afghanistan, his ever-present sense of guilt that Mac had lost his legs and other friends he'd served with in the army who had lost their lives.

'I don't suppose you want to hear all this stuff,' he'd said gruffly one day the previous week when he'd glanced at his watch and discovered that their meeting had overrun by two hours.

'You should talk about what happened to you in Afghanistan instead of bottling it up.' Arianna's gentle reply had made him feel raw inside, and the temptation he felt at every one of their meetings to take her in his arms and kiss her soft, inviting mouth almost overwhelmed him.

He wondered when she had changed from the spoilt heiress with a scandalous reputation in the press to the hard-working, funny, compassionate woman he had got to know. And then it occurred to him that she hadn't changed, that this was the real Arianna Fitzgerald, and the shallow socialite he had believed her to be when he'd been assigned as her bodyguard had only existed in the tabloids.

Santino brooded over this one Friday evening, four days before Christmas, as he drove through an area of London that had the dubious honour of being known as the most underprivileged borough in the capital. The problem was Arianna herself. Or, more specifically, his obsession with her. He thought about her all the time and it couldn't continue. Having an affair with her seemed the only solution. Admittedly another solution would be for him to take a step back. He could appoint one of his executives at Tiger Investments to teach her about business and marketing instead of doing it himself. His chief finance officer had a Master's degree in economics. But he'd seen the way that James Norton looked at Arianna. The guy practically salivated over her. Santino flexed his hands on the steering wheel when something hot and corrosive unfurled in the pit of his stomach.

He did not understand the possessiveness he felt for Arianna, and the truth was it unsettled him. In the past, women had come and gone from his life leaving no mark on him. He had enjoyed their company fleetingly, enjoyed the sex more, and had never thought of them again after the affair ended. Which brought him full circle, he brooded. The solution to his problem with Arianna was to sleep with her. When they were together in his office he had noticed the loaded glances she sent him when she thought he wasn't looking at her. Their sexual chemistry had always been off the chart, but in Sicily he had held back because he'd felt responsible for her.

Following the directions on the car's satnav, Santino parked in a narrow street lined with Victorian houses that had evidently been turned into flats. He checked the address that the butler at Lyle House had given him when he'd gone to Kensington, hoping to find Arianna. He'd had to cancel their usual Friday morning meeting because he had been delayed on a business trip to Germany. Their next meeting was scheduled for when he returned from New York after the Christmas break. His excuse for wanting to see her was so that he could discuss a promotion idea. But he had been informed by the butler that Arianna had moved out of her father's house when she had returned to London from Italy at the end of the summer.

Some youths swigging lager out of cans were hanging around the front door. They eyed Santino suspiciously, but his height and build gave him an obvious advantage, and they stepped back to allow him to pass. Loud rock music pounded from one of the flats, and his mouth thinned as he clambered over a ripped-open rubbish bag on the stairs on his way up to the top floor.

Arianna opened the door when he knocked and looked cautiously round the safety chain.

Her eyes widened when she saw him. 'What are you doing here?'

'I was going to ask you the same question,' he said tersely as he followed her into the dingy bedsit. There was a bed, a sofa and an old television in the main room and a tiny kitchen and shower room off the passage. 'Why are you living in this dump?'

She shrugged. 'It's all I can afford. Rents in London are astronomical and I was only able to afford the deposit on this place with some money I inherited from my grandmother. I pay the rent for my design studio from my business account, but the money you have invested in my business is not for my personal use.'

'I don't expect you to live here,' he said grimly. 'Why did you move out of your father's house?'

'Because I want to be free from Randolph's attempts to control my life. No one will be able to accuse me of relying on my father or using his money to establish my business. It's important that my fashion label Anna is completely independent from Fitzgerald Design.'

He prowled around the cramped room. When

he glanced at Arianna, the wary expression in her eyes threw him back to Sicily, when she had crept around Casa Uliveto like a timid mouse. Guilt twisted in his gut as he acknowledged that he'd been excessively harsh because he had felt honour-bound to fight his desire for her.

'Did you want something?' she murmured. 'Only it's late, and I was about to go to bed.'

Her hair was piled on top of her head and a few stray, damp curls framing her rose-flushed face were an indication that she had recently showered. He lowered his eyes to the man's shirt she was wearing and wondered if she was naked beneath it. The oversized shirt came down to mid-thigh, and Santino felt a lick of heat run through him as he let his gaze roam over her long legs. He wanted to feel them around his hips. He badly wanted to press his mouth to the fragile line of her collar bone and undo the buttons on her shirt one by one so that he could cradle her bare breasts in his hands.

'Come to New York with me for Christmas,' he said abruptly. His jaw tightened when she looked startled, and part of him wondered what he was doing. But another part of him that was uncomfortably hard beneath his jeans seemed to be in control of his thought process.

'I—I can't,' she faltered. 'I've made other plans for Christmas.'

Acid seared his insides. 'What kind of plans? Or perhaps I should ask who you will be spending Christmas with. Is it the lover whose shirt you wear in bed?'

The gold flecks in her eyes flashed but she replied coolly, 'Jonny gave me a few of his shirts that he was throwing out. He knows I find them comfortable to sleep in. Not that it is any of your business, but I don't have a lover.'

'I had dinner with a client at The Dorchester on Tuesday night, before I flew to Germany, and I saw you there with Jonny Monaghan.' Santino's breath whistled between his teeth as he remembered how he had been tortured by the idea that Arianna had spent the night at the hotel with the aristocratic Englishman.

'Jonny is my oldest friend. Again it is not your business, but he has been in love with Davina for years.' She put her hands on her hips and her eyes challenged him from across the room. 'You know quite well that it was my first time with you. To be honest, I haven't felt tempted to repeat the experience with anyone else after that unsatisfactory encounter.'

'Unsatisfactory?' The word felt like a slap and he clenched his hands to stop himself for reaching for her.

'Well, yes, frankly. I don't know about you but the earth definitely didn't move for me.' Beneath her flippant tone there was something else that made Santino furious with himself. He'd known that he had hurt her and now he saw the proof in the faint tremble of her lips before she pressed them tightly together. 'I don't know what you want,' she said in a low tone.

'Don't you?' He was unaware that he had moved towards her, drawn by some force of magic that he could not resist. He was so close to her that he could feel the warmth of her skin from her recent shower. The evocative scent of her perfume made him feel drunk with desire. He watched her eyes darken when he stretched out his hand and removed the clip from her hair so that her chestnut curls tumbled around her shoulders. She did not resist him when he pulled her into his arms.

'Then let me show you,' he growled against her lips before he covered her mouth with his and kissed her as he had longed to do since he had put her on a plane in Sicily.

Arianna knew she should not open her mouth to Santino's demanding kiss but she couldn't help herself. It was madness, but she didn't care. Months of missing him so much that it had been a permanent ache in her heart, and the last three weeks of frustrated longing for his touch, meant that she was helpless beneath the onslaught of his passion. The fierce glitter in his green eyes revealed a hunger that he could not hide. The hard length of him pressed up against her pelvis made her arch into him, needing to be even closer to the power and glory of his muscular body.

She told herself it was the shock of his unexpected visit that clouded her judgement and made it impossible for her to think when her entire being was focused on the feel of his lips sliding over hers. When he pushed his tongue into her mouth she shook with a need that only this man had ever evoked in her. She slid her arms up to his shoulders, anchoring herself to his strength while her heart soared.

His kiss was everything she had dreamed of on the lonely nights since she had left Sicily. He was everything she wanted—so handsome it hurt her to look at him, so strong and yet so exquisitely gentle as he feathered kisses over her cheek and nuzzled the sweet spot behind her ear.

Her breasts felt heavy and molten heat pooled between her thighs. He tasted like heaven and when she held his face between her hands the rough stubble on his jaw felt abrasive against her palms. He sank a hand into her hair and clamped his other arm around her waist as he lifted her off her feet and carried her the short distance over to the bed.

'I want you,' Santino said hoarsely. 'And I know you want me. Your body betrays you so beautifully, *cara*.' He ran his hand down the front of her shirt and unerringly found the hard point of her nipple. She shuddered when he rubbed his thumb over the taut peak. But the arrogance she had heard in his voice sent a chill through her as she remembered how he had rejected her with brutal indifference.

What kind of a fool was she to allow herself to be so vulnerable again? Where was her self-respect that she had fought so hard for?

She stiffened and pulled out of his arms. 'I do want you, it's true,' she said huskily. It was pointless to deny it after she had kissed him so eagerly. 'But I'm fairly certain, taking into account my limited knowledge of these things, that I don't want sex without strings. I'm sure it works for some people, but I waited until I was twenty-five to lose my virginity, and I want something more than casual sex.'

The stunned expression on Santino's face would be hilarious, Arianna supposed, if she didn't feel like crying. If she achieved nothing else in her life, at least she could claim the accolade of being the only woman to have turned him down. It didn't feel as good as she might have thought.

He made a frustrated sound. 'What are you hoping for, Arianna? A declaration of love?'

His tone was scathing. 'Or are you holding out for a ring on your finger?'

She gave his questions serious consideration. 'Not the first necessarily, and then only if it was an honest declaration. As for marriage...' She grimaced. 'My parents' miserable attempt at marriage was not a good advertisement. I stopped believing in fairy tales a long time ago. But friendship, mutual liking and respect are things I will hope for in any relationship I might have.'

'I do respect and like you,' he insisted. His tone was so grim that he might have been announcing the outbreak of a war. 'But I don't wear my heart on my sleeve, and I have no intention of ever falling in love.'

Arianna tried to ignore the pang her heart gave. 'Why not?' She wished she knew what he was thinking but his chiselled features gave nothing away. 'What are you afraid of?'

He swore. 'Love is a pretty word for lust. What we have going on between us is real and honest.'

His hands reached for her again and the gentle brush of his fingers down her cheek almost made her weaken. Almost. But she would not respect herself if she succumbed to the hard gleam in his eyes, even though she longed to let him show her how good they would be together. Instinctively she knew that sex with him would be amazing. But she also knew that it wasn't enough for her. It would never be enough. She would want more from Santino than he was prepared to give, and he would destroy her.

She stepped away from him and hugged her arms around herself to replace the warmth of his touch when he dropped his hands down to his sides. 'I think you should leave,' she said huskily. A spurt of pride made her repeat the words he had said to her in Sicily. 'We'll forget that tonight happened.'

His eyes glittered. 'I'll go, if you are sure that's what you want. But I won't ask you again, *cara.*'

She stared down at the threadbare carpet when she heard him open the door. The sound of it closing brought her head up and she ran across the room and pressed her cheek against the wood, listening for his footsteps on the stairs. The silence stretched her nerves and she was tempted, so very tempted, to fling the door open and call him back. She would love to spend Christmas with him in New York instead of alone in her horrible bedsit. Since moving out of Lyle House, she'd been on a steep learning curve about how to fend for herself. A little part of the old Arianna longed for the luxurious lifestyle she had taken for granted. But she could not allow Santino to save her. She had to save herself.

Finally she heard him walk across the landing and the thud of his footsteps on the stairs faded away. Arianna continued to stand with her palms pressed flat against the door, telling herself that she had done the right thing to send him away. But it felt like a hollow victory.

Christmas was hectic, and Arianna spent the first few days of the New Year moving into her new design studio off Bond Street. The premises comprised a large workroom on the upper floor with a showroom below. She was glad to be busy so that she did not have time to think about Santino. But at night she lay awake, torturing herself with visions of him enjoying the festivities in New York with some gorgeous and no doubt sexually experienced woman—or women.

She missed their meetings at his office, which usually extended to them having lunch together. He was generous with his time when he explained business strategies to her, and his marketing ideas were quite brilliant. It was easy to see how he had become a millionaire tycoon, although she suspected that the real key to his success was his stubborn determination and a willingness to work eighteen-hour days. He had admitted that his busy schedule left little time for a private life, and Arianna wondered if it was an excuse to avoid personal relationships.

Why couldn't she just accept that he did not want a relationship with her? she asked herself angrily. Instead of mooning over him like a lovesick teenager, she needed to focus on establishing her fashion label. She was excited about her new studio. The bigger workshop meant that she had been able to employ a seamstress and pattern cutter, while in the store she stocked a range of ready-to-wear clothes and offered a personal consultancy service. The rent on the premises in a prime central London location was exorbitant, but Santino had advised that she needed a visible presence in order to attract high-end customers.

She wished he were here with her for the opening day of the Anna store, but she hadn't heard a word from him since he had stormed out of her flat ten days ago. She missed him desperately and asked herself why she had turned him down, when all she wanted was to be in his arms—and in his bed, she admitted. She could not forget the wild passion that had blazed between them in Sicily. Although Santino had pulled back, she was certain that the fire had burned as hotly for him as it had for her. But he had felt responsible for her when he'd discovered that she was a virgin. She *should* have told him, she thought guiltily.

The jangle of the bell over the door sent her hurrying through from the back office into the store, thinking that she had her first customer. But instead she was handed a delivery by a courier. Mystified, she opened the box and discovered an exquisite winter bouquet of white lilies, pale lilac-coloured freesias and delicate snowdrops. The perfume of the freesias in particular filled the room with a heavenly fragrance.

With the bouquet was an envelope, and Arianna's heart missed a beat when she pulled out an invitation to a charity fundraising dinner and ball at a top London hotel as the plus-one of Mr Santino Vasari. The event tomorrow evening was being hosted by the prestigious Society of Business Entrepreneurs, and she told herself that Santino must have asked her to accompany him because he had a financial stake in her business.

She turned the invitation over and read the few words written in his bold hand on the back.

I will pick you up from your studio at seven p.m.
Please come.
Yours, Santino.

Her breath caught in her throat as she wondered why he hadn't simply signed his name.

She warned herself not to read too much into why he had written 'yours' when he patently wasn't hers. But when she had put the flowers in water she propped the invitation against the vase and smiled every time she looked at it.

By the following evening she was a mass of nervous tension. Santino hadn't phoned during the day to check if she would be going to the ball, and his arrogance—she supposed that he'd assumed she would jump at the chance to go on a date with him—made her question what she was doing.

It made sense for him to collect her from her new business premises, as it was near to the hotel where the event was being held. Arianna was wearing another of her own creations: a strapless black velvet ball gown with a tight-fitting bodice and a full skirt overlaid with black and silver tulle. Once again, the dress bore the hallmark of her romantic, fairy-tale designs. Her hair fell in loose curls, caught back from her face with a narrow velvet ribbon, and there was a sparkle of diamonds at her throat.

She stopped fiddling with her hair when she

heard the ring of the doorbell, and her heart was thudding painfully hard when she ran downstairs from the studio and invited Santino into the store.

'Hello,' she said breathlessly, blushing when she realised how gauche she sounded. Like a teenager on a first date rather than the sophisticated woman she wanted him to think she was. He looked mouth-watering in a tuxedo, and she could see through the fine silk of his white shirt the dark shadow of his chest hairs.

He let his gaze roam over her, and the fierce glitter in his green eyes set her pulse racing. *'Bellissima,'* he said softly.

She pretended to misunderstand him and lifted her hand up to her necklace. 'They were my grandmother's diamonds.'

His sexy smile stole her breath. 'I wasn't sure if you would come.' His oddly rough tone eased her doubts and she smiled back at him.

'I'll just get my coat.'

'Wait. Give me your wrist.' He slid his hand into his jacket pocket, and Arianna tensed when he fixed a diamond bracelet around her wrist. It was an exquisitely delicate piece of jewellery, and she was aware of how much it must have cost.

She bit her lip. 'I can't possibly accept this.'

'It's your Christmas present, and also an apology for behaving like an ass the other night.' He hesitated, his eyes narrowing on her face. 'Did you have a good Christmas?'

'A busy one. I volunteered at a homeless shelter and lost count of how many portions of plum pudding I served up.'

He was still holding her wrist, and moved to capture her hand, lifting it up to his mouth and pressing his lips against her fingers, sending a shockwave of heat through her. 'I wonder if anyone knows the real Arianna Fitzgerald,' he said wryly. His husky voice caressed her senses like a velvet cloak as he murmured, 'I'd certainly like to be given the chance.'

Did he mean it? While she was trying to formulate a reply he took her coat from the hook and held it while she slipped it on. The frosty night air cooled her hot face when she followed him out to his car.

'Did you have fun in New York?' she asked in a determinedly casual voice as he drove them to the hotel. 'I suppose you went to loads of parties?'

'Not one, as it happens. I stayed with my sister and her fiancé. Gina is in the early stages of pregnancy, and suffering from morning sickness, so I was roped in to cook the lunch. Immediately after Christmas I flew to Devon to visit my grandparents and try to persuade my grandfather to employ someone to help him on the farm. He is nearly eighty and still milks the cows by himself.'

'Will you take over the farm one day?'

He shook his head. 'I suppose it will be sold eventually, unless Gina decides to take it on. The plan had been for my parents to run it, but after my mother died Dad had no interest in anything and spent the next ten years drinking himself to death,' he said grimly.

They had arrived at the hotel and there was no chance to continue the conversation. But Arianna had heard an emptiness in Santino's voice that made her realise how hard it must have been for him as a teenager, when his happy family had been torn apart by the loss of his mother, and because of his father's decline into depression and alcoholism. Perhaps it explained his aloofness, she mused. The deep affection in his voice when he spoke of his sister showed that he did have emotions, but he kept them under tight control.

Arianna had attended many high society functions, but it was hard not to be impressed by the hotel's magnificent banqueting room, which had been decorated with stunning floral displays. Five courses of the finest food were served at dinner, but she was too aware of Santino sitting beside her to do justice to the meal. She drank a little champagne, but the bubbles of excitement inside her were caused by the smouldering glances he sent her, and the brush of his thigh against hers beneath the table burned through her dress.

After dinner there were speeches by representatives of various business organisations and from the heads of the charities that would receive money from the fundraising event. Santino excused himself from the table—Arianna assumed to visit the restroom—and she was surprised when he walked onto the stage.

Standing behind the podium, he explained

that he had set up a charity that provided help for injured ex-servicemen and women to find jobs. The charity, called Can Do, offered practical training in new skills, along with psychological support for people living with the mental and physical effects of war. Santino spoke movingly about his co-founder Mac Wilson, who had lost his legs in an explosion, and of the many other service personnel who had been invalided out of the armed forces and needed to find new careers.

Later, in the ballroom, he drew her towards him, one hand resting on her waist and the other at the small of her back as they danced together. The music tempo slowed, and Arianna's heart raced when Santino pulled her even closer and she felt his lips brush across her brow. Their bodies moved in complete harmony, and with a soft sigh she gave herself up to the music, the moment and the intriguing, infuriating, irresistible man who was holding her in his arms as if she were infinitely precious.

She did not want the night to end, she acknowledged when the ball finished at midnight, and they were in the car driving through the brightly lit city streets. Perhaps he had read her thoughts and he shot her an intent look. 'Do you want to come back to my place for a drink?' he murmured.

She took a swift breath that did nothing to slow the frantic pounding of her heart. Instinctively she knew that if she declined his invitation he would not put pressure on her, but it would be the last time he'd ask her.

What did she have to lose? whispered a voice in her head. Sexual chemistry had fizzed between them all evening, and the way that Santino had been so attentive and charming hadn't been an act. His desire for her was there to see on his gorgeous features and in the burning intensity of his gaze. He was no longer her bodyguard. She understood that his sense of honour had stopped him from making love to her when they had been in Sicily. But now she did not need his protection.

They had pulled up at some traffic lights and she turned towards him, her eyes finding his in the dark car. 'All right,' she said steadily. 'But I've had enough to drink for one night.'

His slow smile sent a quiver of anticipation through her. 'We will have to think of something else to do then, *cara mia.*'

CHAPTER TEN

Arianna expected Santino's apartment to be as minimalist and edgy as his black-and-chrome office in The Shard. But his penthouse close to Tower Bridge was a stylish yet comfortable home, with beautiful wooden parquet floors and muted gold soft furnishings that reminded her of Casa Uliveto in Sicily. The huge bi-fold glass doors that ran the length of the apartment looked over the river Thames and across to the historical Tower of London.

'Let me take your coat,' he murmured, coming up behind her as she stood in front of the window and pretended to study the view of the city lights reflected on the black river. She allowed him to draw her coat from her shoulders and watched his reflection in the glass as he placed it over the back of a chair. He slipped off his jacket and bow tie and unfastened several of his shirt buttons, revealing an expanse of olive-gold skin and a scattering of black chest hairs.

The spicy scent of his aftershave made her senses tingle and a shiver prickled over her skin when he came back and placed his hands on her bare shoulders. The heat from his body was tantalising and she was aware of the inherent strength of his broad chest when he drew her against him. She felt the solid ridge of his erection press against her bottom, and her insides melted. His warm breath feathered along her collarbone as he murmured, 'Have you changed your mind about that drink?'

She sensed he was not going to push her into anything she did not want to do and that he was waiting for a sign from her. Pulse racing, she turned around to face him. 'I haven't changed my mind,' she told him huskily. 'I don't want a drink. I want you to make love to me.'

Something feral and fierce blazed in his eyes but he said in a measured voice, 'I don't do love, *cara*.'

The warning was loud and clear: *Don't ex-*

pect more than I'm prepared to give. And she wouldn't, Arianna assured herself. She would abide by Santino's rules. But she knew she would regret it for the rest of her life if she didn't explore the feelings he aroused in her, the hunger that coiled tight and hot in the pit of her stomach. She stood on her tiptoes and brushed her lips over his. 'Then show me what you *do* do,' she challenged him softly.

'*Dio!* You drive me insane.' The rasp of his voice sent flames across her skin as he pulled her into his arms and lowered his head. He claimed her mouth with a possessiveness that caused her heart to slam into her ribcage as he slid a hand beneath her hair to cup her nape, and angled her head so that he could plunder her lips.

The hunger in his kiss dissolved the last of her doubts. She sensed the moment his iron control snapped, and met the demands of his mouth with demands of her own as their scorching passion ignited into an inferno.

'You are so beautiful,' he said hoarsely when he lifted his lips from hers and trailed hot kisses along her jaw, then down her throat, moving lower still to explore the slopes of her breasts above the neckline of her dress. Her nipples were tight and hot, and she shuddered when he ran the zip down her spine and freed her breasts from the velvet bodice, cradling her firm flesh in his palms.

She arched backwards in mute supplication, offering her breasts to him, and could not restrain a gasp of pleasure when he closed his mouth around one taut peak and laved it with his tongue, before moving to do the same to her other nipple. The sensation of him sucking each rosy tip in turn evoked an ache in her pelvis, a primal need that consumed her and made her impatient for him to assuage the throb between her legs.

'Do you have any idea how many nights I have been kept awake by fantasies of doing this?' he growled. 'I wanted you with me in New York.'

'I wished I'd gone with you,' she admitted. 'I want you to show me everything, Santino.'

He swore softly and pulled her zip all the way down so that her dress pooled at her feet in a froth of black and silver tulle. His eyes glittered as he studied her slender body, naked except for her tiny black silk panties and sheer black hold-up stockings with bands of lace around her thighs.

'Beautiful,' he said again, in a low tone that resonated with desire, before he scooped her up in his arms and carried her through to the bedroom. Arianna barely noticed the ultra-masculine décor of brown and gold. She only saw the huge bed as Santino tossed back the covers and laid her down on the cream satin sheets. She watched him strip off his clothes and felt a sharp tug of anticipation in the pit of her stomach when he pulled his boxers down his hips and his erection jutted thick and hard from the mass of black hairs at his groin.

The bedside lamps emitted a golden glow that highlighted the angles and planes of his face and gave a sheen to his bronzed skin. He was a work of art, so handsome that she felt weak looking at him, and weaker still as she imagined him driving his solid shaft inside her.

'I want to touch you,' she whispered when he knelt over her. She ran her hands over his chest, and explored the ridges of his powerful abdominal muscles, but when she skimmed her fingers over the tip of his arousal he groaned and captured her hand.

'Not this time, *cara*. I want you too badly.' Sitting back on his haunches, he slid one stocking down her leg, followed by the other, and then hooked his fingers into her panties and pulled them off. His eyes gleamed as he pushed her thighs apart and ran his finger over her opening, his mouth crooking in a sexy smile when he put the same finger into his mouth. 'You taste sweet,' he murmured, returning his finger to her moist folds, gently parting her so that he could slide in deep. All the while he trapped her gaze with his, and the feral gleam beneath his half-closed lashes made her heart thunder.

'Do you like it when I do this?' He rotated his finger inside her until she gasped and trembled, and then he slipped a second finger into her, moving his hand in an erotic rhythm while she curled her fingers into the sheet and made a guttural sound in her throat.

'Please,' she croaked. She was a slave to his mastery as he caressed her with consummate skill, flicking his thumb over the sensitive nub of her clitoris so that she arched her hips towards his hand, desperately seeking something that she sensed was near yet was frustratingly elusive.

When he withdrew his fingers from her, she felt a flicker of dread that he was about to reject her again. She closed her eyes, unable to bear the humiliation she had felt in Sicily.

'Arianna, look at me,' he bade her, his voice like rough velvet. Swallowing hard, she obeyed him and her heart missed a beat at the intensity of his gaze. 'I have never wanted anything in my life as much as I want you right now,' he said, and it was as if he was making a vow. She watched, dry-mouthed, as he unrolled a condom over the length of his erection, and understood why he had stopped caressing her momentarily. Her pulse rate accelerated when he lifted himself over her and nudged her legs open with his thigh.

And then he pressed forward so that the tip of his manhood pushed slowly, so slowly, into her as he claimed her inch by exquisite inch, filling her with his hardness. The size of him made her catch her breath, and he waited, his eyes burning into hers, while her internal muscles stretched to accommodate his powerful penetration.

'*Sei mio,*' he muttered, his mouth against hers, before he kissed her with an eroticism that made her tremble anew as he tangled their tongues. Distantly in her mind she seemed to recall that the Italian words meant 'you are mine'. But then he withdrew from her a little way, and she lost the ability to think as he thrust deep and repeated the action again and again.

He took her with long, steady strokes and increased his pace when she lifted her hips to meet each devastating thrust. He drove her higher, higher, and she dug her nails into his back as the pressure inside her built to a crescendo. His mouth claimed hers again and the unexpected tenderness in his kiss crept around her heart.

'Let go, *cara mia,*' he whispered at the same time as he slipped his hand between their sweat-slicked bodies and unerringly found the tight nub of her femininity. The effect was shattering, the caress of his clever fingers combined with the relentless rhythm of his possession sending her up and over the edge. She cried out as she flew into the flames and burned. The intensity of her orgasm was indescribable, and when moments later Santino gave a harsh groan and collapsed on top of her, his big body shuddering in the throes of his climax, Arianna felt their souls connect as profoundly as their bodies were entwined.

Santino rolled onto his back, breathing hard, his heart still pumping like a piston in his chest. He had known that sex with Arianna would be good. The chemistry between them had always been white-hot, and all it had taken was one spark to set off an explosive reaction.

Initially he had been driven by his piqued male pride to demonstrate that there was nothing *unsatisfactory* about his skill as a lover. But somewhere along the way her ardent response, coupled with a faint uncertainty that revealed her inexperience, had blown him away. He'd found that he could not control his urgent desire. His blood had pounded in his veins, and when he'd entered her and felt how tight she was he had almost come right then. It had never happened to him before, and in the aftermath of their wild passion he wanted to understand why Arianna's mix of innocence and sensuality turned him into putty in her hands.

Not quite putty, he thought self-derisively as he felt himself harden again. A ripple of tension ran through him. He'd had the best sex of his life with Arianna. But it was just sex, he reassured himself. His emotions were not involved, nor would they ever be. He had learned when he was a teenager that he was better off alone. Safer.

He turned his head and studied her when she sat up. The flush of rose on her cheeks was repeated on the tips of her breasts where his mouth had suckled her. He ached to curl his tongue around her pouting nipples, but the wariness in her big brown eyes stopped him from reaching for her. She lifted her hand to push her tumble of silky curls back from her face and the diamond bracelet twinkled in the light from the bedside lamp.

'You should only ever wear diamonds, *cara*,' he murmured, running his finger over the sparkling stones around her neck, before he cupped one breast in his hand and succumbed to the temptation to close his lips around its tender peak. The faint gasp she gave fuelled his desire even more and he frowned when she swung her legs over the side of the bed.

'I should go.' She scooped up her knickers and dress from the floor, and stood there looking decadently sexy and oddly vulnerable, holding armfuls of tulle. 'Taxi drivers often refuse to drive along the street where I live after midnight. Apparently it's a no-go area controlled by drug dealers.'

'I don't want you to go back to your flat tonight.' As he spoke, Santino decided that he did not want her to live in a notoriously rough part of London. He would find a place for her closer to his apartment, somewhere with a good security system and a concierge. His thoughts raced ahead. When this thing he had with Arianna had burned itself out, he argued with himself, he would still want her to live somewhere where she would be safe.

'You are not my bodyguard and I am not your responsibility,' she told him firmly. He recognised the glint of battle in her eyes and realised that she needed careful handling. Throwing back the sheet, he walked over to her, his heart contracting when he noted the pink stain on her cheeks deepen as she seemed transfixed by his unashamedly naked and aroused body.

'You said you wanted me to teach you everything,' he reminded her softly as he took her dress from her and threw it onto the chair before he lifted her into his arms and carried her back to bed. 'We have barely started your lessons, *cara mia*.'

'Oh.' Her eyes widened when he laid her down on the sheet and proceeded to take a condom out of its wrapper and roll it down the length of his erection. 'Do you... Do you want to do it again?'

That husky uncertainty in her voice was going to kill him, Santino decided. 'What do you think?' he drawled, kneeling over her so that his swollen tip pressed against her moist opening. He shoved her legs wide apart. She bit her lip and the beast inside him growled.

'I think I'm ready for my second lesson.' Her tremulous whisper increased his urgency. But, just to be sure that she was absolutely ready for him, he bent his head to the feminine heart of her and bestowed an intimate caress with his tongue that had her writhing as she sank her fingers into his hair. 'Please...' she moaned when at last he positioned himself over her.

She was so beautiful lying there with her legs open, utterly exposed to his hungry gaze. As he slid his shaft between her silken folds and drove deep inside her, he felt again the odd sensation of a hand squeezing his heart. But then she wrapped her long legs around his back, as he had so often imagined her doing, and he pushed everything out of his mind as he gripped her hips and began to move, taking them both to the edge of ecstasy, and they flew into the fire together.

Afterwards she curled up against him while her breathing, and his, gradually slowed. When she tried to move away he clamped his arm around her waist. 'Stay,' he murmured, 'and in the morning I'll cook you breakfast.'

She stretched like a sleepy kitten. 'All right,

but I need to take my necklace off. The clasp is delicate and I'm worried it could break.'

He unfastened the clasp and dropped the string of diamonds into her hand. 'It clearly means a lot to you. Were you fond of your grandmother who gave you the necklace?'

'I adored her. Grandma Charlotte died when I was twelve, a year after my mother went away. She was the only person who understood that my brattish behaviour was a result of missing my mum when she moved to Australia without me. I felt confused and angry.'

Santino remembered that he had felt those same emotions after his mother had died. 'Surely your mother came back to visit you, or you visited her?'

'No. My father paid her to stay out of my life and I had no contact with her until earlier this year. When we did finally meet again, we were strangers.'

While Santino went to the bathroom to deal with the condom, he found himself wondering if any of the tabloid editors who had labelled Arianna a spoilt socialite knew or cared that her childhood had been unhappy, despite the wealth and privilege she had grown up with. The hurt in her voice, when she'd spoken about her mother who had abandoned her and her father's indifference, made him furious on her behalf.

Returning to the bedroom, he was unsurprised that she had fallen asleep. It was two a.m., and he had been awake since six the previous morning, but he wasn't tired. Arianna made him feel alive in a way he had never felt before. He did not make a habit of asking his lovers to stay the night, but he couldn't find it in him to regret her presence in his bed when he slid in beside her and she immediately curled up against him. Her glorious hair rippled over the pillows and her long lashes made dark fans on her cheeks. Tomorrow he would deal with the complicated emotions she aroused in him and lay down some ground rules, he promised himself. But for now he was content to draw her soft, curvaceous body against him and count her eyelashes one by one.

When Santino woke the next morning it was to an empty bed and, he quickly discovered, an empty apartment. Checking his watch, he was astounded to find that it was nine forty-five. He never slept in. Even on the rare occasions when he asked a woman to stay over, he was always up early for an hour in the gym before his morning shower—his usual routine. Invariably he was keen not to prolong the night before for longer than he could help, and he was adept at evading awkward questions about future dates.

But Arianna had left without waking him or even leaving a note. As he slammed around the kitchen making coffee, he told himself he should feel relieved that she obviously understood the no-clinging and no-crowding rules that he insisted on in an affair.

Two cups of strong black coffee and a shower later, his mood had not improved and, when he arrived at his office and glared ferociously at a junior secretary who spilt a jug of water over his desk, he called Arianna simply to make sure she had got home safely.

'I'm at my studio. I had to unlock the store this morning to let my assistant in,' she explained in an airy voice that made him grit his teeth. 'I didn't want to wake you when I left your apartment.'

He waited for her to ask when they would see each other again, or at least drop hints that it would be lovely to meet up. 'Look, I have to go.' She sounded distracted. 'I'm about to have a consultation with a client who wants several outfits for a cruise she is going on.'

'Have dinner with me tonight?' he said quickly. 'I'll pick you up from the studio at seven.'

'I can't I'm afraid.'

Santino's jaw clenched. Was she playing games, playing hard to get? And, if so, why wasn't he prepared to walk away? There were plenty of other attractive women he could invite to dinner. But there was only one Arianna, and she was the only woman he wanted, he acknowledged.

'A client is coming for a fitting at seven-thirty this evening because it's the only time she has available, but I should be free by nine o'clock, if you want to meet me then,' Arianna told him.

Some of the tension drained out of him. 'I'll see you at nine.'

'Okay.' Her voice became husky. 'I think I will be ready for my next lesson by then.'

Dio! He stared at his phone when she ended the call, not sure if he wanted to swear or laugh. She was a minx, and he spent much of the day devising suitable punishments, which involved him kissing every single inch of her body while she writhed and pleaded for his possession.

By nine that evening, when Santino parked his car outside the Anna store, he had got himself back under control, and he was determined to take control of his affair with Arianna. She would have to understand that he called the shots in their relationship—which wasn't even a relationship. They shared an intense physical attraction, but passion like theirs couldn't last, and he gave it a month before it burned itself out.

Her assistant seamstress was just leaving when he entered the shop, and after the woman had gone he locked the door and walked up the stairs to the design studio. Despite the late hour Arianna was still working and Santino paused in the doorway to admire the sight of her delectable derriere covered in tight black jeans as she bent over one of the big cutting tables. She must have heard his footsteps and she spun round, pushing a wayward curl off her face and giving him a wide smile that did odd things to his insides.

'Guess what?' she said, dropping her dressmaker's scissors and running across the room to launch herself at him. He laughed as he caught her in his arms, fascinated as ever by her spontaneity. Her perfume teased his senses and he pressed his face into her hair as she wrapped her legs around his hips. 'I had two new clients visit the store today and they placed orders for dresses. You were right about the importance of a visible presence on the high street. I wouldn't have the Anna store and design studio without your financial support through Tiger Investments.'

She tipped her head back and the gold flecks in her brown eyes glowed. 'You look very macho in black leather,' she murmured, running her hand over his old biker jacket. 'What will you do if I kiss you?'

The tug of desire in his groin was so sharp it made him catch his breath. 'Why don't you find out?' he said thickly, and couldn't restrain a low groan when she covered his mouth with hers and kissed him with a sensuality that made him shake with need. 'Do you have any idea what you do to me?' he muttered against her throat while his fingers deftly unfastened the buttons on her pink silk blouse. The black bra beneath it was semi-transparent and her dusky pink nipples were visible through the sheer material.

She pressed her pelvis up against his painfully hard erection as he carried her over to the worktable, moving her hips sinuously to create a burning friction between their bodies. 'I have some idea,' she murmured and caught her breath when he sucked her nipples through her bra.

'Good, then you will understand that I have to have you now. I can't wait, *cara*.' He set her on her feet and swiftly dispensed with her blouse and bra, cradling her bare breasts in his palms and flicking his thumbs over the taut peaks. He had never felt such an intensity of need as he did with Arianna.

A warning voice inside Santino's head reminded him that he was supposed to be in control and establishing the rules and boundaries of their affair, but he shoved the thought away and slid his hand into the stretchy material of her jeans, rubbing his fingers over the panel of her panties and then slipping inside them to caress her wet heat.

Arianna was breathing hard, and when he eased back a fraction he saw that her eyes were half-closed and her mouth slightly open, her pretty face flushed with passion. 'I want you too,' she whispered, placing her hand on the bulge of his arousal beneath his jeans. 'But how can we do it here?'

'Like this.' He kissed her hard on her mouth and then turned her round and gently pushed her down so that she was bending over the table.

'Santino?' She looked over her shoulder at him, her eyes wide with excitement and faint uncertainty that he was anxious to dispel.

'It will be good, baby, trust me.'

'I do trust you,' she said softly, and something fierce and unexpectedly tender tugged in his chest. He feathered kisses down her spine and then gripped the waistband of her jeans, pulling them and her knickers down her hips. She kicked off her shoes and he helped her to step out of her trousers before he ran his hands greedily over the smooth, pale contours of her bottom. Hand shaking, he freed his rock-hard erection from his jeans and nudged her thighs apart. He surged into her, feeling the faint resistance of her vaginal muscles at first as he drove in deep and filled her.

It was wilder and hotter than anything Santino had ever experienced, but it could not last. Jaw clenched, he held her hips tightly while he established a devastating rhythm, faster, harder, the soft moans of pleasure she made shattering his tenuous control. He thrust again, and her thin cry mingled with his harsh groan as they climaxed together, and the power of it sent shudders of aftershock through him.

Afterwards he held her in his arms and claimed her mouth in a slow, deeply sensual

kiss that somehow seemed even more intimate than the mind-blowing sex they had just
shared.

'You're coming back to my apartment tonight,' he told her after he'd driven her back
to her bedsit and clamped a protective arm
around her shoulders as they walked past the
gang of youths hanging around the front of the
building. 'You can't possibly like living here,'
he said when she looked mutinous.

'I don't like the flat or the area,' she admitted. 'But at least I am independent of my father. Hopefully my label will start to sell and
I'll be able to afford a nicer place to live.'

'You can take a salary out of the money I
have invested in your business to pay for your
living costs. In the meantime you need to stay
with me so that we can continue your lessons,'
he murmured, pulling her into his arms and
kissing the pout from her lips until she melted
against him.

After she had packed a bag he took her back
to his penthouse, and while she had a bath he
ordered Thai food from his favourite restaurant. Of course, the sight of her all pink and

flushed, smelling divine after her bath, aroused a different hunger in him and he had to have her again. It was nearly midnight when they finally ate the food straight out of the plastic containers it had been delivered in.

'This is fun,' Arianna said happily as she sat cross-legged on the sofa, eating noodles as gracefully as if they were dining at a five-star restaurant. Her smile faded and Santino discovered that he would give away everything he owned if he could put the smile back on her lips.

'What's the matter, *cara*?'

'Oh, there was a spiteful piece written about me in one of the fashion magazines. You would think I'd be hardened to bad publicity by now,' she said flatly, revealing a vulnerability that made his insides clench. 'But the journalist who wrote the article suggested that my father is the creative and financial force behind Anna and Randolph must help me with the designs.'

He rubbed a hand over his jaw. 'We need to devise a great PR campaign in the run-up to London Fashion Week. You could give a couple of interviews to explain your concept of Anna as a fashion brand for contemporary women. It would also be a good idea if we gave a joint press statement about Tiger Investments' involvement in your company.'

'Would you be prepared to do that?'

He nodded. 'I have a vested interest in wanting Anna to succeed as I own a forty percent share of the business,' he reminded her. 'Leave the PR campaign to me while you concentrate on producing a runway collection that will blow the fashion world away.' He untied the belt of her bathrobe and cupped her breasts in his hands. 'But right now I think you should concentrate all your attention on me,' Santino said thickly as he scooped her into his arms and carried her back to his bed.

CHAPTER ELEVEN

ARIANNA'S KNEES ACHED from kneeling on the floor in front of a mannequin while she sewed the hem on a cocktail dress that she planned to include in her collection at London Fashion Week's spring show. Her back was stiff, her fingers were sore from sewing sample pieces—her seamstress could not do all the work alone—and with less than a week to go until the show she was beset by self-doubt.

After weeks of preparation, the actual amount of time during which her designs would be paraded on the runway by the models she had hired was minutes. But she knew that those moments could make or break her fledgling career. Fashion editors, writers and bloggers would scrutinise her work and their verdict of her debut collection was crucial to the future of her Anna label. She wanted to succeed as a designer, not just for herself, but to prove to Santino that the faith he had shown by investing in her business had been justified.

'I thought we agreed that you would not work past 9:00 p.m.' Santino's gravelly voice had its usual effect on her heart, making it flutter like a trapped bird in her chest. She removed a couple of pins that she'd been holding between her lips before she stood up and turned to see him stroll across the studio. He had changed out of the suit that she'd watched him put on that morning into black jeans and a grey cashmere sweater topped by his black leather biker's jacket that gave a dangerous edge to his devastatingly sexy looks.

'I just need to finish this,' she explained, grimacing when he shook his head.

'No, *cara*, you need to come home for some food, a relaxing bath and bed.'

A shiver of pleasure ran through her at his use of the word 'home'. Technically, of course, the penthouse near Tower Bridge was Santino's home, but for the past month she had lived there with him. She was still paying the rent on her bedsit, while she was supposed to be looking for a new flat to move into, but she had been so busy preparing for the fashion show, and the few places she had viewed online hadn't met with Santino's approval.

If she was not careful she would start to believe that he was as happy with their current living arrangements as she was, Arianna thought. Her good sense warned her not to hope he felt something for her that went deeper than the sex-without-strings affair he'd insisted was all he wanted. But when he smiled at her the way he was doing right now, and when he kissed her with passion and an inherent tenderness that played havoc with her heart rate, she dared to wonder if he might love her a little. It would be too good to be true, because she loved him a lot. With all her heart, in fact. The voice in her head that cautioned that she could get badly hurt was way too late.

She glanced back at the mannequin. 'The show is in three days and I still have tons to do. It will only take me another five minutes to finish this. I'm not tired,' she insisted.

'All the more reason for us to have an early

night,' he drawled, with a glint in his eyes that caused her stomach muscles to clench with anticipation.

As it was, they did not even make it to the bedroom at his apartment. He pulled her into his arms and kissed her hungrily while the lift took them from the underground car park up to the penthouse. Once inside, they tore each other's clothes off, and he tumbled her down onto the sofa and made love to her with a fierce intensity so that she shattered once, twice, before he let out a harsh groan and collapsed on top of her.

It was early the next morning when Arianna woke with a start to the sound of Santino shouting. She sat up in bed and switched on the bedside lamp. He was sprawled next to her, the sheet tangled round his hips, his head moving restlessly on the pillow. His eyes were closed and he was breathing hard so that his chest rose and fell jerkily. When she touched his shoulder his lashes flew open and he stared at her blankly.

'You were having a nightmare,' she told him softly.

He shoved a hand through his hair. 'I'm sorry if I woke you.'

She bit her lip. His desperate cries had ravaged her heart. 'Was it about when you were serving in Afghanistan?'

'No.' He exhaled heavily. 'I was dreaming about my father.' Arianna waited, and after a moment he said roughly, 'I've mentioned before that after my mother died Dad sank into a deep depression and became reliant on alcohol.' A nerve jumped in Santino's cheek. 'One evening he disappeared from the house. I knew he'd been drinking all day, and I was worried when I couldn't find him. I went down to the beach that had been a favourite place he used to go to with Mum.'

'Did you find him?'

'Yes, I found him. He had walked into the sea fully clothed. It was winter and the waves were huge. By the time I waded into the sea, he had been under the water for a few minutes and he was a dead weight. I was scared that we would both be swept against the rocks but I finally managed to drag him back to the beach, and he punched me.'

'He *punched* you? Why?'

'Because I'd saved his life. He wanted to die and be with my mother.' Santino's jaw clenched. 'He loved her so much that nothing else mattered to him, not his children or his business. For my father, death was preferable to living without the woman he loved.' He gave a grim laugh. 'What does that say about love?' he asked savagely. 'When I was a boy I looked up to my father, respected him. But I watched him become a pathetic drunk. Love weakens and destroys.'

Arianna stared down at the sheet that unconsciously she had been pleating between her fingers. 'Perhaps that's true for some people, but for others love strengthens and empowers them,' she murmured.

She took a deep breath, aware of the painful thud of her heart beneath her ribs. Santino's story made her ache for him, for the teenage boy who had risked his own life to save his father. His mother's death had robbed him of both his parents and it wasn't hard to understand why he had a deep mistrust of strong emotions.

But she was sure he felt something for her. They had grown so close these past few weeks, and every time they made love it felt like a complete union that was much more than the physical act of sex. Hearing what had happened in his past gave her an insight into why he kept tight control of his emotions, but the fact that he had opened up to her surely must mean he trusted her?

'Love has made me stronger,' she said softly. 'I love you, Santino.'

'Then you are a fool,' he bit out coldly. 'I made it clear from the start that all I wanted was a no-strings affair.' His green eyes were as dark and wild as a stormy sea. 'Whatever romantic notions you have about me are a fantasy. I don't believe in happy-ever-after, and I am not in love with you.'

A knife sliced through her heart but she clung desperately to hope. 'You can't deny that we have been happy these past few weeks,' she said huskily.

'Sure, we have amazing sex, but it won't last.'

'Only because you don't want it to last.' She put her hand on his arm. 'I understand...'

'No, Arianna, you don't get it.' He shrugged off her hand and swung his legs over the side of the bed. She watched him yank open the wardrobe and grab a T-shirt and jogging pants. 'It was always going to end between us because I can't give you want you want. I don't want to fall in love with you or anyone else.'

His words fell like hammer blows, smashing her dreams to pieces, but she was not prepared to give up on him, on them. What she had learned since she had vowed to take charge of her life eighteen months ago was that you had to fight for what you wanted.

'I know you love your sister,' she argued. 'I think you are afraid to allow yourself to fall in love with me. You're scared to give us a chance.'

'There is no *us*,' he told her curtly. He had pulled on his clothes and strode over to the door. 'I should have guessed that you would want more.' His voice was as hard and uncompromising as the expression on his granite features. 'Women always do.'

Arianna stared at the door after Santino had slammed it behind him, feeling numb. His parting shot played on her deepest insecurities—his implication that she was one of a long list of women he'd had affairs with who had hoped for more from a relationship with him than he was willing to give. She had no idea where they went from here. But, having given him her heart and had it thoroughly trampled on, she could not bear to be humiliated by him again—and she could not continue to live in his apartment.

Tears stung her eyes but she angrily blinked them away. The old Arianna might have curled up in a ball and cried, but she had a fashion show to put on, a business to run and, she remembered with a jolt, she and Santino were supposed to be holding a joint press conference later that day to promote her Anna label. She could take the easy way out and make up an excuse for why she couldn't attend. But *she* was not a coward, she thought grimly.

She bit her lip. Santino was a war hero and

couldn't be accused of cowardice, which must mean that he had told her the truth when he'd insisted that he wasn't in love with her. She must have imagined she'd seen a tender expression in his eyes that had given her false hope.

His PR team had arranged for the press interview to be held in Tiger Investments' hospitality suite. Arianna felt sick with tension at the prospect of seeing Santino again, but her pride insisted on her hiding her broken heart. As she had done so often in the past, she disguised her feelings behind a wall of bravado, and when she sauntered into his office—wearing a scarlet suit with a very short skirt and four-inch heels, black patent stilettos that made the most of her shapely legs—she had the satisfaction of seeing dull colour streak along his cheekbones.

'You're cutting it fine,' he said brusquely as he glanced at his watch, and she had a strange feeling that he was desperate for an excuse to look away from her. 'The interview is at twelve, and it's five to.'

No way was she going to admit that she had arrived at The Shard fifteen minutes ago and had paced up and down the cloakroom trying to control her nerves. Santino held open the door, and as she walked past him the evocative scent of his aftershave almost made her crumble. But she lifted her chin and gave a confident smile to the group of journalists assembled in the hospitality suite.

She sat down on a sofa facing the journalists and tried not to stiffen when Santino sat next to her. She'd prepared a short speech outlining her ideas and aspirations for her fashion label, which she delivered perfectly without glancing at her notes.

'You stated that your only financial backing comes from Tiger Investments and that your father, the celebrated designer Randolph Fitzgerald, has no involvement in your fashion label,' a journalist said.

Arianna nodded. 'That's right. Anna is entirely independent from my father's fashion business.'

'That is not entirely true,' the journalist persisted, looking at Santino. 'Isn't it the case, Mr

Vasari, that you were given a significant number of shares in Fitzgerald Design by Arianna's
father when his company was floated on the
stock exchange last summer?'

'No, you have been misinformed...' Arianna
began.

Beside her Santino shifted in his seat.

'Yes, I received shares in FD when it became
a public company.'

Arianna's stomach hit the floor.

'So there is a link between Randolph Fitzgerald and Anna.' The journalist gave Arianna a
triumphant look. 'Mr Vasari owns shares in
your father's company and Tiger Investments
provides financial backing to your business.
Did your father give Mr Vasari the shares to
persuade him to back your fashion label? And
is Randolph in fact the creative genius behind
Anna?'

'Absolutely not,' Santino answered the journalist tersely, but Arianna barely heard him.
Her head was pounding and she felt horribly
sick at the shocking news that Santino had
shares in Fitzgerald Design. She pressed her

hand to her brow, feeling as though her head was about to explode.

'Arianna, are you all right?' Santino asked urgently. His fake concern battered her already bruised heart.

'I have a migraine. I'm sorry, but I can't continue with the interview.' She lurched to her feet, and hurried out of the hospitality suite. She flinched when Santino caught up with her and put a hand on her arm. Anger joined the host of violent emotions swirling inside her and she couldn't hide her sense of betrayal. 'Don't touch me, Judas,' she hissed, before she spun away from him and stalked down the corridor with her head held high and her heart in tatters.

A cruel wind whipped across the Devon beach where, twenty years ago, Santino had dragged his father out of the sea. He shoved his hands deeper into his coat pockets as he stood, watching the waves crash onto the shore. White spray flew up and mingled with the mist that slicked his hair against his skull, but the freezing temperature was not as cold as the lump of ice in his chest.

He was sure he would never feel warm again, that he would never smile again. For what was there to smile about when he had lost the one thing in his life that he cared about more than anything else—the one person who had briefly melted the ice inside him and filled him with light and laughter?

'Arianna.' He whispered her name and the wind whipped it away. He could not forget the shock and devastation on her face when the damned journalist at the press conference had revealed that he had accepted shares in her father's fashion business. *Dio*, he should have seen it coming and prepared her. It should not even matter. The journalist had made more of the link between his interests in Fitzgerald Design and Anna than really existed. He had not kept the shares, and had donated them to the charity he had set up. But Arianna did not know that, and she hadn't given him a chance to explain. He knew he had hurt her badly, perhaps even more than when he had brutally rejected her for a second time.

He rubbed his hand over his eyes and discovered that his lashes were wet. It must be the mist or the salt spray from the sea. These could not be tears sliding down his cheeks, he assured himself. As he walked along the beach, the mournful cries of the wheeling gulls echoed the silent cry of pain inside him. Had his father felt this miserable when he had tried to drown himself all those years ago? Santino halted and kicked a lump of sand with the toe of his boot. His father had wanted to die rather than face life without the woman he loved. Now *he* was facing a lonely, pointless life without the woman who had captured *his* heart.

Arianna's accusation that he was scared to fall in love with her taunted him. He had been commended for his bravery when he'd served with the SAS in Afghanistan, but in truth he was a coward. Since he had been a teenager he had supressed his emotions and turned his back on love. But where had that got him? Santino asked himself painfully. He was alone on an empty beach and hurting like hell. He did not want to walk into the sea. There was only one place he wanted to be, only one woman he wanted to be with. As he tore back up the beach, he could only pray that he hadn't left it too late finally to come to his senses.

The days leading up to London Fashion Week were crazier than Arianna could have imagined. It was a good thing that she'd had no time to eat or sleep because she didn't feel like doing either. Since she had walked out of the press conference and away from Santino, her appetite had been non-existent. Luckily she had been so exhausted from dealing with last-minute preparations and problems for the show that when she had crawled up the stairs to her bedsit at night she'd slept for a couple of hours without dreaming of him. But his treachery was the first thing she remembered when she opened her eyes, and her heart felt like a lead weight in her chest.

Tonight she should be feeling on top of the world and celebrating at one of the celebrity-packed parties she had been invited to. But instead she was alone at her studio, where she had escaped to after the show. Her runway collection had received a standing ovation and

Anna was the buzz word on the lips of every fashion editor, blogger and fashionista.

Such recognition and excitement for an emerging brand was unusual and she felt proud of her debut presentation. But it all felt mean- ingless without someone to share her success with. Jonny had been at the show with Davina and some of her other friends, but the only person she longed to see had not been there. Santino's absence had reinforced the message that he wasn't interested in her.

Arianna stiffened when she heard footsteps on the stairs. She was sure she had locked the shop door, and only she and Santino had a key. She whirled round and her heart collided with her ribs as she stared at him.

'You look terrible,' she burst out. 'What's happened?' His face looked ravaged. There was no other word to describe the deep grooves on either side of his mouth and the tormented look in his eyes as he walked towards her. There was only one person he cared about. She swallowed. 'Is it your sister? Has some- thing happened to the baby?'

He shook his head, his gaze riveted to her

face. 'Gina said that her pregnancy is progressing fine when I spoke to her an hour ago. She told me that I'm an idiot, but I already knew that.' He halted in front of her and raked his hair off his brow with an unsteady hand. 'The fact that you can show so much compassion after everything I have done is proof, if I needed it, that I am the greatest fool in the world.'

He did not really look terrible, of course, she acknowledged as she raked her eyes greedily over him. He looked dangerously gorgeous in faded jeans, a black sweater and the leather jacket that she loved almost as much as him. Arianna looked away from him and released her breath slowly. 'I don't understand, and to be honest I don't really want to. I'd like you to leave.'

Something almost desperate flashed across his hard features. 'Will you at least listen to me? And then you can throw me out if you want. God knows, it's nothing more than I deserve.'

Stupid tears filled her eyes and she blinked them away angrily. 'Did my father give you shares in Fitzgerald Design to persuade you to be my bodyguard?'

He held her gaze unflinchingly. 'Yes.'

She choked back a sob, devastated anew by his betrayal. 'You should have told me when I applied to Tiger Investments for funding for my fashion label. You *knew* how important it was to me that Anna was in no way linked to my father.'

'I didn't keep the shares,' he said quietly. 'Initially they were paid into Tiger Investments' accounts but I transferred them over to the charity I set up to help ex-servicemen train for new careers. No link exists between your fashion company, my investment company and your father, and I have given a statement to the press to that effect.'

'You know what some journalists are like. They would love to see me fail,' she said bitterly. 'They won't believe that the clothes in the Anna brand are entirely my designs, and they'll think that my father must have something to do with my company.'

'The fashion editors I spoke to after your

presentation at London Fashion Week were in raptures over your work.'

She stared at him. 'How do you know?'

'I was there. Of course I was there,' he said softly. 'I was so proud of you this evening, Arianna. You are incredibly talented and you work damned hard. You deserve to be the huge success that I am confident you will be.'

His praise only made her heart ache even more. 'If you were at the fashion show why didn't you come and join me? I wouldn't have had the chance to take part in the show if you hadn't invested in my business.'

'Tonight was your night and I wanted you to enjoy the acclaim.' He hesitated and a nerve in his cheek flickered. 'I was scared to approach you in case you told me to go to hell,' he said roughly. 'I am a coward as well as a fool, and I couldn't face the possibility that I might have driven you away for good.'

'I thought that was the plan. You wanted to drive me away.' She couldn't hold herself together. Seeing Santino again was tearing her apart and a tear slid down her cheek. 'You could not have made it any clearer that you don't feel anything for me,' she whispered.

'I love you.'

Another tear slipped down her cheek, and another, and another. She didn't know what hurt most—his lie, for it *must* be a lie, or the terrible darkness in his eyes that made her think, made her hope, that he actually meant it.

'You don't do love.' She threw the words he had said to her back at him. 'You want to go through life untouched by emotions, unloving and unloved.'

'I love you,' he repeated, his voice thick, as if his throat was constricted. His eyes were fiercely bright and her heart stopped when she saw that his lashes were wet. 'I know what I said, and for a long time it was true. I didn't want to feel the level of emotions that had destroyed my father. But then I met you, Arianna.'

His hand shook as he reached out and brushed a stray curl back from her face. 'The most beautiful woman I have ever seen. I took one look at you and my wonderfully ordered, controlled existence was blown apart. You infuriated me with your defiance and captivated me with your loveliness, which I quickly discovered is much more than skin-deep. You are beautiful all the way down to your compassionate heart.'

Her mouth trembled. 'How can I believe you? You sent me away—*twice*. You broke my heart, Santino. I spent most of my life wishing that my father would love me and it nearly broke me. I can't do that again.' She scrubbed her wet eyes with the back of her hand. 'If you can't love me the way I want to be loved, the way I love you, then I'm better off without you.'

'*Tesoro mio*—' His voice cracked. 'If you give me the chance, I will spend the rest of my life showing you how much I love you. You are everything, Arianna—' he swallowed convulsively '—and without you I am nothing.'

Hope unfurled inside her, a tentative happiness that she wondered if she could dare to believe in. 'Truthfully, you love me?' she whispered.

'Perhaps this will convince you.' He slipped his hand into his jacket pocket and pulled out a small velvet box. Her heart juddered to a halt when he opened it to reveal an exquisite cluster of diamonds set on a white-gold band. 'I had better do this properly so that you can tell our grandchildren the story of when I proposed,' he murmured as he dropped down onto one knee.

'Santino,' she said faintly.

'Will you marry me, Arianna? Will you have my babies, and will you love me for ever, as I will always love you?'

More tears slipped down her cheeks, but they were tears of joy as she looked into his eyes and saw the blaze of emotions in his glittering green gaze. 'I don't know what to say.'

'Say yes, *cara mia*,' he pleaded, 'and make me the happiest man in the world.'

Arianna smiled and heard him catch his breath. 'Yes,' she said softly, holding out a trembling hand for him to slide the engagement ring onto her finger.

'I said you should always wear diamonds, and now you always will,' he murmured as he stood up and drew her into his arms. His mouth claimed hers in a kiss that stirred her soul with its tender devotion.

'I love you.' She looped her arms around his neck as he lifted her off her feet. 'I think you should make love to me right now.'

Santino's soft laugh was husky and hesitant, as if he too could not quite believe that love was theirs for the taking, theirs for all time. 'Try and stop me, baby,' he murmured against her lips. And then he worshipped her with his body so beautifully, so *lovingly*, that Arianna discovered fairy tales could come true.

* * * * *

LET'S TALK
Romance

For exclusive extracts, competitions
and special offers, find us online:

- **f** facebook.com/millsandboon
- ⓞ @millsandboonuk
- 🐦 @millsandboon

Or get in touch on 0844 844 1351*

For all the latest titles coming soon,
visit millsandboon.co.uk/nextmonth

Want even more
ROMANCE?

Join our bookclub today!